A Time To Begin

Tricia Linden

Kingsburg Press

San Francisco, California

Kingsburg Press
P.O. Box 475146
San Francisco, California, 94147
www.KingsburgPress.com

A Time To Begin is a work of fiction. Names, characters, places, and incidents are a product of the author's imagination. Locales and public names are sometimes used for atmospheric purposes. Any resemblance to actual people, living or dead, or to businesses, companies, events, institutions, or locales is completely coincidental.

Editor: Barbara Millman-Cole
Cover Design: Killion Group
A Time To Begin / Tricia Linden – 1st ed.
ISBN- 13:978-1-946177-00-1
ISBN- 10: 1-946177-00-8
eBook ISBN: 978-1-946177-01-8

Other Works by Tricia Linden

The MacNicol Clan Through Time

A Time To Return – Book 2

A Time To Belong – Book 3

A Time To Forgive – Book 4

.

.

.

Dreaming In Moonlight

.

.

.

Jules Vanderzeit novels

set in the Gilded Age of New York

Until We Meet Again

Until Their Hearts Desire

.

Coming Soon: Until You Love Me

Dedication
To Susan N. of my Spiritual Sisters Book Club.
Thank you for the blessing of your love and support.
And to Romance Lovers Everywhere.

CHAPTER 1

Sophie liked nothing better than a good story, especially ones with happy endings, but enough was enough. Too irked and irritated to listen to any more of Adam's stories, she left the banquet room in a huff and fled to her room, shutting the door behind her. Finally! What a blessed relief to be away from the annoyingly exasperating crowd paying homage to the queen's favorite suitor. Adam loved to capture everyone's attention with tales of his earthly adventures, but Sophie was tired of his never-ending boasting.

Pooh on Adam and his stupid, boring stories. So what if he had ventured out into the earthly realm and mingled with humans? Why should she or the rest of the fae kingdom care? Pooh on her sister Danu, the queen of the fae, for being so delightfully entertained by his ramblings. Even pooh on her sister Sindi for laughing at his tales and encouraging him to tell more. But mostly, pooh on her for not having her own stories to tell. Nothing exciting ever happened to her.

Feeling frustrated and angry, Sophie stepped over to the large floor-to-ceiling windows standing open to the breeze and stared off into the distance, ignoring the beauty of the verdant lawns, lush trees, and brilliant blue sky stretched out before her. Too agitated to sit still, she turned to retrace her steps across the room, pacing back and forth, again and again, until she wore herself out and fell limp on a silk covered divan.

It was annoying to think she had lounged away another day listening to gossip and tall tales from Adam. Still, annoying as he was, Sophie was also intrigued by Adam's stories. What was it about the earthly realm that made it so appealing? Maybe she should take a look for herself. Focusing her mind, she gazed through the veil shielding the world of the fae from that of the humans' to see what she could find. The scene that appeared before her was a rough and rugged seashore with gentle rolling waves. Unfortunately, the splendid landscape was scarred by a lone man lying face down on the beach. *Darn.* It was so like a human to muddy up a perfectly good view of their earth, and yet, offensive as his presence was, she found she couldn't look away.

Unlike many of her friends, Sophie rarely, if ever, peered through the veil to watch the humans go about their puny, little lives. She was the queen's sister, and though the youngest of her siblings, she was too important to lower herself to such trivial pursuits. Humans were known for being distasteful, ugly creatures, surely not worthy of her attention. She'd heard dozens, perhaps hundreds, of stories told by Adam and her friends about their adventures with humans, how they would interact, interfere, and cause mischief with them, but she only considered them silly little stories told for her amusement; certainly none had piqued her interest enough to make her want to join their escapades.

At least not until now. She couldn't help but wonder, why this particular human, lying face down on the sand, had caught her attention and made her look?

Was he handsome? It was hard to tell; he was so beaten and bruised, no doubt from one of those ghastly battles humans were so fond of waging, especially the men. *Stupid idiots.* It was as if they had nothing better to do than run around and think of ways to be cruel and murderous to each other.

Yes, the fae had their wars, heated disagreements really, but they didn't go around sticking sharp pointed swords into each other's bodies; not that it would do much good considering the fae were nearly immortal. Fae used other methods to get their point across, such as the time they locked the people of Fomoire in a mountain for a hundred years. Or the time her father had overrun a neighboring fae kingdom with rabbits until they covered the land; she grinned happily at the memory of his resourcefulness.

More intrigued than she wished to admit, she turned her attention to the man on the earthly beach, thinking she would indulge in another moment or two of uninterrupted time to observe this one particular human who had somehow managed to capture her curiosity.

As she looked deeper into his world and closer at his prone figure, she saw he was indeed a warrior. Scottish, no doubt, based on the dirty hunk of plaid draped about his body, his exposed muscular legs, and the deep cinnamon-red hair covering his head. He might be handsome, once he got cleaned up, but it would take an awful lot to get him back in fighting shape. And for what? So he could go out and get beaten up all over again and eventually killed? Because that's what they did, these temperamental, overly emotional, passionate humans. It seemed they lived only to fight another day.

Perhaps it was the thought of these creatures being emotional and passionate, or the feeling of concern that tugged at her heart as she viewed the dying man, but she was suddenly tempted to wander over to the other side of the veil and see what all the hubbub was about. She was in need of some amusement, and the prospect of meddling with a real, live human rather appealed to her. At least she thought he was still alive. Surely it wouldn't hurt to go and take a look; she would only stay for a minute or two, three at the most. Then later, when she sat at the banquet table with her older sisters and friends, she would have her own story to tell. Wouldn't they be surprised? If for nothing else, it would be worth it to see the looks of amazement on their faces and hear their exclamations of delight.

Sophie stood up from the rose covered divan where she had been lying and adorned herself in a beautiful diaphanous blue gown with layers of whisper thin silk flowing about her body. It was a very nice look. With a wave of her hand, she wove sweet, little wildflowers into the braids holding back her long blond hair that reached to the small of her back. She didn't need to see her reflection in the full-length mirror hanging on her wall to know she looked good, but she looked anyway, and liked what she saw. Any human who saw her would surely know she was fae of the highest order and bow down to her in sweet appreciation of her mere presence in their world.

Oh, this was going to be fun.

~*~

Herrick of the MacNicols was grateful he was still breathing, although he was no longer standing and probably wouldn't be for quite some time, if ever again. After his boat had run aground on the rocky shoreline, the effort to drag himself to this beach had taken nearly all he had. Thanks to the powerful hand of God, he had managed to return to his precious Isle of Skye. Now, if he should die, he held hope that at the very least a compassionate kinsman might find his wretched body and bury his bones, ensuring his soul would be at peace.

Peace, what a blessedly pleasant thought. To be done with the needless, senseless, endless battles his uncle insisted on fighting. And for what? To claim his rights, to show his power, and to prove his possession of the land? With so much fighting, soon there would be no people left to tend the land or for the victors to rule. Clans fighting against clans—it seemed to be the way of life for the Scots. Scots against Scots, Scots against Norse, Norse against Norse—*Hell*, couldn't anyone get along?

How could his uncle have allowed Big Red to pull them along in his get-revenge-quick scheme? Uncle Nicail had gone seeking glory and recognition as a clan chieftain;

but for all his grand designs, he may now be dead, lost on some godforsaken isle ruled by the Norse. What glory was there to be gained in that? Not only had his clan's impulsive leader risked getting himself killed, he had forced his ill-considered plan on his two sons and had taken Herrick along with them.

With shameless gratitude, Herrick had found himself left for dead on the abandoned battlefield. No doubt, his foes had left him there to rot, but their oversight had saved his life, giving him an opportunity to slip away and drag his beaten and bruised arse back to Skye. If he was truly lucky, he'd lived to fight another day. If not, at least he was back on Skye. Three cheers for Herrick—possibly the lone surviving MacNicol of another great Norse Isles war, at least for now. That was still subject to change.

Herrick decided then and there he'd had enough. Never again would his sword be raised in battle except to defend his life and his mother, should the saintly woman still be alive. He could only hope the invading Norse had not been allowed to capture Skye.

When he had been younger, the heat of battle had run hot in his veins and his belief that might equaled right had ruled his thoughts. But now, at thirty summers, he no longer had the taste for battle. He had lost his father, wife, and only son to the wages of clan wars; he would pay no more.

Based on the pain coursing through his limbs, Herrick surmised they were all still attached. As he took stock of his injuries, his body suddenly shuddered and convulsed as he coughed up a soup of seawater, blood, and bile. Fighting against the pain, he spit out the bilge filling his mouth. The gory mess landed disgustingly close to his face, but at least he was no longer at risk of choking on his own vomit.

Ever so slightly, he turned his head—*damn that hurt*—and tried to open his eyes, or more correctly, his eye. Apparently his right—or was it his left—nay, 'twas definitely his right eye that was swollen shut. He thought about the effort it would take to sit up and decided rolling to his side was the best he could do, but then again, why the hell bother. Judging by what he could see with his one good eye—which wasn't much—and the dryness of the ground beneath his body, he had managed to stagger above high tide, which meant he wasn't in danger of getting swept back to sea. Maybe it was best to lie here for another hour or two, or even a day, until his strength returned. In his current condition, he had neither the might nor the willpower to swat a fly, much less start a fire or seek shelter, all things needed to keep him alive.

He was about to close his eyes again and allow himself to drift back into the black nothingness of sleep when he caught sight of a shimmering blue light appearing through the mists of fog shrouding the beach. No longer mindful of the pain throbbing throughout his body, he focused all his attention on the strange, unearthly blue glow. Slowly, the luminous image of a beautiful young woman with long blond hair and piercing sapphire-blue eyes appeared before him.

Holy Mother of God! Herrick realized he was looking into the mesmerizing eyes of a fae.

There was no doubt in his mind; if he weren't already a dead man, he soon would be. He had some knowledge of the fae and their world of magick. 'Twas his belief they were all ruthless meddlers who had nothing better to do than wreak havoc in the lives of men. His only hope was to appeal to her narcissistic sense of power and convince her it would benefit her if she were to let him live.

This wasn't going to be easy, for what benefit could a dying man possibly offer an all-powerful fae?

~~~

Sophie walked over to the human and peered at him in wonder. It appeared he was alive, although from what she had heard about these people, only barely. A whiff of his scent caught her by surprise before she shielded her nose. While everything in this world smelled ghastly, this man smelled even worse. He reeked of sweat and unkempt bodies and other things she could not think to name.

She winced before she remembered who she was and regained her composure. She was the youngest sister of the queen of the fae. She would not be deterred from her adventure; although it occurred to her that perhaps it would have been prudent to have told someone where she was going or even to have brought along a minion to act as guard and servant.

Oh well, too late now to worry about such details. She was here, and she wasn't going to leave until she had a reasonably good story to take back home and share at the dinner table.

Perhaps she ought to reach out and touch him, or poke him, to see how he felt. Humans were supposedly soft and mushy, but this one appeared to be all hard and muscular. She surveyed him from the heels of his feet, up along his long out-stretched legs, lingered a moment at the rounded curve of his buttocks, and finally settled her gaze upon his broad back and bulging shoulders, which were hardened and finely chiseled. Umm, yes, it might be quite nice to get a feel of all that hard muscle, or the nice curve of his buttocks. Sophie crouched down and slowly, cautiously stretched out her hand. She was about to make contact when he suddenly drew a deep breath.

"Stop! Wait!" he shouted.

Startled, Sophie pulled back in alarm and fell on her backside. Oh my, she hadn't expected him to speak. What should she do now?

"Please, wait." He turned his head and then with obvious effort, rolled onto his side. "I ken I'm as good as a dead man, but if ye could grant me one last boon."

Boon? She thought about this word as she scrambled to sit upright. "Do you mean a favor? Like granting a wish?"

His lips took on a slight curve. Perhaps he was attempting to smile. The effort wasn't very successful. He wasn't classically handsome, not like the men of the fae race. His face was too misshapen to be called pretty or handsome, but beyond his swollen eye and matted hair, she saw primal beauty. Under better conditions, he might even be considered good looking. Surprisingly, she sensed an inexplicable attraction when she had expected to only feel repulsed.

"Yes, grant me a wish, if ye please," he said. His voice was rough and husky sounding; much different from the fae.

"Why should I do that?" she asked.

"Because ye can," he stated. "Surely 'tis within yer power."

Sophie liked how that sounded. She would be seen as benevolent and kind, and it seemed quite royal to go about granting wishes and favors. But humans were known for always trying to take advantage of the fae. She needed to proceed with caution. It was probably best if she didn't let him know this was her first venture into the human realm, or that she was truly of royal blood. She smiled at her own cleverness, thinking no human would get the better of her.

"First, you must tell me your wish, then I will decide if I want to grant it." That was very good, she thought, rather pleased with herself; that sounded like something her eldest sister would say.

"My one eye is swollen shut, and I canna see well with the other. All I ask is that ye would heal my eyes so I may see the fullness of yer beauty afore I die."

Oh my, what a very good wish. How could she possibly deny a dying man the benefit of seeing her beauty? It wasn't as if he were going to live to tell anyone about it. Then again, what good would it do to heal his eyes and let him gaze upon her marvelous beauty if he weren't able to live and tell the tale. It was obvious he was in need of greater healing than merely his swollen eye, but she had never healed a whole human before, much less part of one. She wasn't exactly sure how it was done. Of course she had the power to heal, but since the fae folk were so rarely injured, she had never actually put her power to much use.

Oh, this is splendid. Healing the human warrior would add greatly to her story back home. Yes, she would start with his eyes and see how that went, and then if the results pleased her, she might do more.

She knelt down next to him, but not too close; she didn't want to risk that he might reach out and grab her; she wasn't ready to feel the touch of his hands upon her. Once he took a hold of her, it was said, she would be unable to leave until he let her go. Feeling properly positioned, she proceeded to offer him her gift.

After lightly kissing her fingertips, she placed them on his eyelids. She then closed her eyes and sent a pulse of white, healing light through her fingers. When she opened her eyes, she saw his face was awash in the white light, his eyes sparkled, and his smile had become brighter. Maybe she had used too much power. Oh well, there was no taking it back now.

"Did it work?" she asked, feeling like a stupid little elf. Of course it had worked; she was a faerie princess after all.

"Ye are truly lovely," he said in awe. "'Tis as if I can see everything kind and beautiful contained in yer soul. Ye have granted me a most wondrous wish indeed."

11

The way he said it made her feel special, much more special than when one of her fae friends tossed empty compliments at her in hopes of gaining her favor. Vulgar as this man appeared, he seemed genuinely grateful and appreciative of her power. She liked that about him.

"Are you able to sit?" she asked.

He started to push up from the ground. "With yer help, I'm sure I could."

She nodded, "Yes, of course, you *need* my help." How wonderful. Unlike the fawning fae at the queen's palace, this man actually needed her help. Oh yes, this could be quite interesting indeed. "And I shall help you, because I can," she said with a bit of self-importance. "Now let me see, I wonder how I should do this," she mused aloud. Though he had managed to roll onto his back, he still seemed rather helpless.

"Mayhap, if ye grabbed my arms, ye could help pull me up," he suggested thoughtfully.

"Yes, let's see if that will work."

Sophie reached out and placed her hands around his wrists; her slender fingers barely reached around them. He in turn clasped on to her wrists, and she gently pulled him forward until he was sitting upright. As he moved, she noticed he gritted his teeth together and made a small groaning noise. She hoped she hadn't hurt him too awful much and sent another small pulse of white light through her hands, this time with her eyes open. The healing light seemed to help, and she felt his muscles relax somewhat. It seemed they were making progress.

He sat with one leg bent, the knee pointing skyward, and the other still resting upon the ground. Though there was evidence of a nasty looking wound running down his leg, she couldn't help but notice the strength contained in his muscular thighs.

"Yer touch is wondrous indeed," he said, sounding a bit in awe. "I feel better than I have in days. I suspected ye have great power, but this is more than I had hoped."

"Of course my power is great, I am . . ." She stopped herself, thankfully, before she revealed who she really was. If he knew she were the youngest sister of the faerie queen, he might try to take advantage of her, and she could not take such a risk. It was best to let him think she were one of the lesser fae, though it offended her ego somewhat to do so. "I am of the fae, as I'm sure you well know."

He nodded. "So I thought. Ye have granted me a most wondrous boon; to see such a lovely sight as ye helps me to forget my wretched aches and pains."

"Have I really? Have I helped you forget your aches and pains?" This was even better than granting a wish; it seemed her mere presence was having an effect on him. Wait until she told her friends back on Avalee.

"I can honestly say, I am much better than when ye found me. So tell me, my little faerie friend, now that ye have me, what do ye plan to do with me?"

For such a strong and able warrior, she thought she saw a hint of fear flick quickly through his eyes. But perhaps she was wrong; perhaps it was only a trick of the light; for as quickly as it appeared, it was gone.

13

"Oh my, I hadn't really thought that far ahead. I suppose I expected to simply leave you here and return to Avalee, but now that we've met, to do so wouldn't seem right. Is there someplace where I can take you? Are you able to walk on your own?"

"That's a might hard question to answer considering I have not yet proven I am able to stand."

"Oh yes." She had forgotten they were still sitting on the pebbly beach; probably because she had been so caught up with looking at his eyes. Had it been her touch that made them such a brilliant shade of emerald green, or had they always been that way? It mattered not, she supposed, as a gift once given was not taken back. "Are you ready to give it a try?" she asked.

"I think I am. With yer help, if ye doona mind."

"Not at all. You have been very easy to work with, considering you're a human."

"I shall take that as a compliment," he said with a smile, and this time he did a much better job. His lips parted to show a row of straight white teeth, and deep dimples appeared in his cheeks. However, his breath, she noticed, could still stand some improvement.

"Oh, I think you should," she said, "considering I don't hand out compliments very often. You could ask my friends back home except I don't expect you shall ever go there. But here, let's try to get you on your feet."

It would be far better to leave him standing on his own two feet than lying face down in the dirt as he had been when she found him. Yes, she was feeling very kind and generous indeed.

Sophie stood first then helped him to his feet, sending him another small dose of healing white light as she did so. She could feel the draining effect of using her power and began to worry she had used too much. It was a reminder she needed to proceed with caution.

Since this was her first visit to the human world, she had no idea how being here would affect her. She wished she had paid more attention to Adam and the others when they had told their tales of encounters with the humans, especially Adam. He seemed to have the most knowledge of how this world worked, but he was known for being the favorite of the faerie queen, and Sophie resented the attention he sought from her oldest sister. Thankfully, the use of her magic was not as draining as she had feared, although she did feel different from her usual self.

The man seemed wobbly and took a moment to lean upon her before he was able to stand on his own, but other than that, it seemed to go well. He was taller than she had imagined, though it was hard to properly judge a man when he was lying face down in the dirt. Looking up at him from this perspective, he looked fiercer, and stronger too. If she weren't fae, it was very likely he could squash her with his bare hands. But she was fae, born in the royal family, sister of the queen.

Taking a deep breath, the bruised and battered warrior stood straight and bore his full weight on his own legs; but when he attempted to take a step, his hands came crashing back down on her shoulders, seeking her support. It was obvious she was not going to be able to do this alone. She had begun to feel the weakening effects of using her healing power and had no intentions of putting herself at risk for the sake of his health, at least not until she knew where this adventure would take her.

"I think we shall need some assistance. I believe I shall summon a horse to help us; a white one if I can find it."

His brow rose toward his forehead.

Sophie ignored his look of disbelief and reached out with her mind to the surrounding area. She found a number of horses, but none of them were white. Oh well, she would work with what she could find.

"Unfortunately, the best I can do is a handsome gray, but he's really quite large. I am sure he will do just fine."

~~~

Herrick didn't care if the horse were pink or blue. If this fae could truly summon a horse, as she had said, he would be thrilled. The very fact that he was standing next to a woman of the fae race, feeling as good as he did, was amazing enough considering only moments ago he had felt as though he were on the verge of dying. To think she was willing to help him was more than he had expected. However, he figured he wasn't completely out of danger, at least not yet. Very few men had seen the fae and lived to tell about it, and those who did, had very little that was good to say about them. Being still weak and at her mercy made him wary. From what he knew of the fae, they were a finicky lot whose moods could change with the wind.

16

It hadn't taken long for him to realize 'twas his show of weakness that kept her at his side and willing to help. As much as he hated the weakened state he was in, there was no doubt it had been his saving grace, for surely if she had found him hale and hearty, there was no telling what manner of spell she might have cast upon him. Instead, she had used her powers to provide a measure of healing and had indicated she was willing to do more. God bless this woman and the saints above who were watching over him.

Now that he was standing, he was able to fully appreciate how beautiful she was. A hard fist of lust gripped his innards and squeezed. He breathed deeply, holding his yearnings at bay. She had indicated she appreciated his gratitude, but he doubted she would welcome his desire. Still, he took a moment to feast upon the fae woman standing afore him. She seemed to be wearing a gown made of shimmering blue liquid. Silver-blond hair tumbled around a beautiful heart-shaped face with a sweetly pointed chin and gently rounded forehead. Her lips were full, pink, and inviting—they called out to be kissed—and her eyes were the deepest sapphire blue he had ever seen. She was passion wrapped in innocence, and she didn't seem to have a clue as to how deeply she affected him.

CHAPTER 2

Moments later, a large grey war horse appeared on the bluff overlooking the beach and made its way down to where they stood. It stopped a few feet away and knelt on its front legs with its head down, literally bowing to Sophie as a show of respect. Herrick was mightily impressed.

"Our steed has arrived. Where shall he take us?" Sophie asked. She made a slight gesture, and the horse rose from his knees.

"I take it ye plan to go with me."

"I think I must. My adventure is not yet over."

That was fine with him, as long as she proved useful. After several long days of battle, the mere sight of her was a boost to his sense of well-being. He also knew her touch had the power to heal, and he was still a long way from being hale and hearty. Aye, his vision had cleared; there was no doubt of that, for he could see farther and sharper than ever afore. Although he had felt a surge of healing flow from her hands when she had helped him to sit, his legs were still weak, and his right shoulder throbbed from the hard blow he had taken in battle. All of these ills would heal in time, with or without her help, but 'twas obvious she could do much to speed them along if she so desired. He wanted to keep her close; he only hoped it wasn't because he was under the influence of her fae power.

Stroking the horse's neck, she added, "I can't allow it to end here. What would I tell the others back on Avalee? That I got you a horse and sent you on your way? That's not a very exciting ending. No, I need something bigger, something grand to amuse my friends. Where shall we go?"

So that was what this was all about; a story to tell her fae friends back home. He could live with that, he thought ironically, considering he may well have died on this beach without her helpful healing.

"I need to return home, to my clan, if it still exists." The recent battle had been a terrible blow to his kinsmen; he wondered how they were faring. Had the Norse invaded his homeland in retribution, as he feared? Or had MacDonald been able to hold them off?

"Where was your home when you last saw it?" the fae woman asked.

"Near Portree, on the eastern side of the island."

From what he knew of the area, he believed he had made landfall on the far side of the island; a hard three days journey home if he were to make it on foot. With a horse, they could easily make it in two.

But it was getting late. He doubted they would make much progress this day afore darkness fell and it became too dangerous to travel. Although he still carried his broadsword at his side and had a dagger hidden in his boot, he would feel a whole lot better if they could find shelter afore the sun set.

Herrick wondered what tricks this little lass possessed to ward off the chills of the night; the gossamer gown she wore looked none too warm. And he expected his stomach would soon be rumbling with demands for food.

"We should leave this beach and be on our way afore we lose our sunlight. I hope ye are not opposed to riding bareback."

"Why must my back be bare to ride this horse?" the faerie asked, looked delightfully perplexed.

He pressed his lips tightly together, resisting the urge to laugh. "Ye misunderstand. I was referring to the horse's bare back. We doona have a saddle."

"Oh! Do horses normally tend to roam the countryside wearing a saddle? Perhaps I should summon one of those."

"Nay, my lass, unless they are being ridden, they doona usually carry a saddle. Come, let me help ye mount."

"Then who will help you?"

"If I can stand, I can mount a horse," he assured her.

"Very good. I am glad to know you are capable of some activity."

"Oh, I can assure ye, my sweet little faerie, there is much activity I am capable of."

"Wonderful. I'm hoping to see what more you can do," she said innocently.

Herrick shook his head with a grin and held his thoughts in check. It would not bode well to let his fantasies run rampant with this little faerie.

"Since we are to be traveling companions, 'twould help if we knew each other's names. How may I address ye?" he asked.

She paused for a moment before she said, "You may call me Sophie, I suppose, since that is my name. Perhaps you should call me Lady Sophie, as a show of respect. Yes, I think I would like that."

"As ye wish, Lady Sophie. I am Herrick of the MacNicol clan." He stood tall and gave her a slight bow.

"Herrick you say! I never would have thought. You seem more like a Stephen, or perhaps a Jonathan, not that I have much experience with these things; but actually, now that I've said it, I do believe Herrick fits you best."

"I certainly hope so, for that 'tis what I have been called all my life." Herrick wasn't a royal name, like James, Jonathan, George, or Stephan; his was a warrior's name, and he believed it suited him well. His father had claimed he was named for an old Norse warrior, a champion who had led men into battle, and there were times when Herrick wondered if his father hadn't been a wee bit overly grand in choosing a name for his only son.

Herrick took a look at the horse standing placidly at the faerie's side. 'Twas a large animal, one well suited to the task of carrying two people, but a horse straight from the field posed a few problems. "We can make do without a saddle, but we should at least have a rope of some sort so we may guide the horse."

She looked from him to the horse and back again. "That won't be necessary. If we tell him where to go, he will go. If we tell him when to stop, he will stop. Where do you want to go?"

"I suggest we take the path that leads south and head inland to where we can find shelter," he said, pointing to where they should go.

She glanced at the horse then said, "Yes, so we shall. He knows the way."

That was pretty darn convenient, Herrick thought.

It took a bit of effort, but Herrick was able to mount the large grey war horse with a tolerable amount of pain and then pull Lady Sophie up to sit in front of him. The feel of her curvaceous backside and long sinuous legs draped across his nearly caused him to moan in pleasure. He was sorely tempted to run his hands over her body, to feel the swell of her breast and cup her backside that curved so fittingly next to him, but he resisted. Such inappropriate actions could easily land him face down in the dirt once again.

While he would usually keep his pains hidden—never let yer enemy know yer weakness—around Sophie he was inclined to be a wee less cautious. He told himself it was his weakened condition that had drawn her to him, and he needed to use her concern to his advantage. He also needed to find the right balance. If he were to show too much weakness, she might lose interest, and yet, it seemed important he show signs of improvement. However, if he were to show too much strength, as if he didn't need her any longer, or worse, was seen as a threat to her safety, it could easily cause her to flee back to her side of the veil. For some reason, that idea didn't sit well with him.

Thanks to the healing she had already applied, he was perfectly capable of making his way home alone, be it on foot or on a horse, but he wanted to keep her near. He told himself it was because he had need of her power—he was interested to see what all she was capable of—but a part of him recognized he simply liked having her near.

He wondered if she had used some type of spell or glamor to make him feel this way. He certainly hoped not. Herrick was fairly confident that wasn't the case based solely on her words and deeds. She appeared as a sweet, naïve, woman-child out on her first grand adventure, and it seemed she wanted to make the most of her time afore she was required to return home. Very likely, if she lingered too long, she would be missed, and someone would come looking for her. She didn't seem like the type who lived alone and took care of herself. Her preference for being called Lady Sophie was a clue to her rich if not royal stature.

She had referred to her home as Avalee, and although he had never heard the realm of the fae called such afore, he wasn't surprised. The Tuatha de Danann were known to be a secretive folk, preferring to remain hidden from view and often working their *magick* in the dark of night or by the light of the moon. Never afore had he heard of a faerie appearing in the light of day.

Herrick wrapped his arms around her to grab hold of the horse's mane and better hold her in her place. It might be an unnecessary gesture, but he felt a fierce need to protect her, especially from the harsher realities of his world. The world of humans would not be an easy place for someone so unacquainted with the earthly realm. Skye and the surrounding islands were full of mean spirited men who would do their best to hurt or take advantage of her in the most horrific ways, and he wanted to protect her for as long and as well as he could. Considering she was fae and had powers far beyond anything he could provide, his desire to protect her might seem unreasonable, even foolish, but ugliness in any form could easily leave its mark on one as young and innocent as she. Practical or not, he would do his best to keep her safe.

Soon they were riding south, as he had requested, winding their way towards the lands of the clan MacLeod. Up ahead was a wooded area where they could find shelter and take their rest for the night. It was nearing twilight, and cold gusts of wind blew in from the sea. Herrick began to worry that Lady Sophie was too poorly clothed for the drop in temperature. When he looked down to ask how she was faring, he saw she was snugly wrapped in a thick cloak of royal blue wool with a fur lining. He grinned begrudgingly.

"It must be nice to conjure up whatever ye need, whenever ye need it," he said with chagrin.

She turned her face to look at him with a mischievous smile. "Yes, it is. Would you like me to summon a cloak for you?"

"'Tis not necessary," he replied, drawing his plaid tighter around his shoulders. He was used to the unending chill carried in the winds of Skye.

"Perhaps not necessary, but surely preferred. Would you prefer to be alive or dead? Would you prefer to ride or walk? Would you prefer to be warm or cold?"

"I believe ye have made yer point," he said begrudgingly. "A bit of warmth would be preferred and greatly appreciated."

She smiled, and he suddenly felt the warmth of a cloak hanging about his shoulders. The thick woolen garment was dark, charcoal grey and edged in fur, much like hers. He was accustomed to enduring whatever nature could dish out, but he had to admit, it felt darn nice to have protection from the cold. "Thank ye, my lady," he said curtly, acknowledging her gift. 'Twas already one of many, and although she'd been nothing but kind, her casual use of magick made him feel disturbingly vulnerable to her power.

"You are most welcome." She turned to look at the road they were traveling and asked, "Have you been here before?"

"Aye, I have lived on this island all of my life and seen most of it at one time or another."

"Why were you on that beach? What happened to you before I found you? Were you attacked by ruffians? Or were you in some type of war?"

He wasn't surprised she had begun pelting him with questions. 'Twas to be expected. "I was returning home from a battle on the Isle of Harris. The MacDonalds requested the help of my chieftain, and I was among the MacNicols gathered to fend off a raid of invading Vikings. Ye could say I was forced to offer my sword in service to assist in their cause, along with a few others."

"What happened to the others? Did they stay on the Isle of Harris?"

He hesitated a moment afore answering, causing her to turn to look at him. "Unfortunately, I canna say. I was knocked out during the battle," it was the blow that nearly blinded him, "and when I awoke, the fighting had moved on. I fear many may have been killed in battle." He stared ahead, not meeting her eyes.

"But you survived. How is that?"

"I was gravely wounded, as ye saw when ye found me, and had been left for dead on the battlefield. When darkness fell, I managed to slip away and was lucky enough to find the boat we left moored on the beach. It took everything I had, but if I were to die, I wanted it to be on Skye."

"Oh," she nodded with a shiver. "That's right; you humans are weak and prone to dying."

"Whereas the fae are strong?" While her magick was strong, she appeared as only a wisp of a girl.

"We can live for hundreds of years, as you count time; however, I am considered young among my folk. I am the youngest of seven sisters, and as you may have guessed, this is my first visit to your world."

"Aye. I thought as much. I hope yer visit is a pleasant one."

He caught a hint of a smile, or was it a smirk, afore she turned to face forward again.

"Interesting, I would say, but not pleasant. Oh, there are some very pleasant aspects to be sure, but it is cold and damp here, whereas Avalee is always warm and pleasant."

"So ye conjured up a cloak." Giving into temptation, he wrapped his arm around her waist, pulling her close, as she sank deeper into the folds of the heavy garment.

"Yes, I *summoned* two cloaks," she corrected him. "One for me and one for you. Where do you think we should stop for the night?"

Twilight was upon them; it was time to find a suitable location to camp for the night. The wind coming in off the ocean had picked up, and the mists covering the isle had turned into drizzle.

"We are headed for that stand of trees near the stream feeding the loch; they will provide shelter and I hope something for our supper."

"Supper sounds nice. What did you have in mind?"

"If I am so lucky, mayhap some fresh fish from the loch." He had gone hungry many nights and would do so again if need be, but he had a suspicion she wouldn't allow that to happen.

"Fresh fish sounds nice, and perhaps some wine and cheese to go with it. And some grapes. I am in the mood for grapes. Will that work for you?"

"Certainly, if ye can find them," he said with a grin. She was an ingenuous little elf, and yet her enthusiasm cheered him.

27

"I am certain I can find anything I want. I only need to put my mind to it."

"Is that how ye found me?"

"No, not exactly. You were simply there, and I felt like an adventure. And now we are here, and I am enjoying myself. Thank you, Herrick of the MacNicols."

"Ye are truly welcome, and I wish to thank ye, my Lady Sophie."

"I've already granted you one wish; you'll not be getting another," she said laughingly.

The sound of her laughter seemed magical, like the sound of a bubbling brook splashing its way through a meadow, or a child at play with its mother. Herrick hoped he could make her laugh often.

When they reached the stand of trees growing along the loch, Herrick said, "I think we should stop here." As soon as he spoke, the horse came to a stop.

Impressed, he wanted to test the limits of how the horse would respond to his voice commands. "Or mayhap further down the path we may find something better. We should continue on a wee bit further," he said.

As instructed, the horse began to walk down the path. A dozen yards later, Herrick said, "This is far enough. I think this will do." The horse stopped again.

Sophie turned to glare at him. "Are you satisfied with your little test?"

Herrick made no attempt to hide his grin. "Aye, my lady. Yer steed has performed most admirably."

She gave him a tight smile. "I am glad you are pleased."

After he dismounted, she let him help her down from the horse then turned to survey their surroundings. "His name is Raynor; it might help if you use it. It means mighty fighter. Rather fitting, don't you think? I imagine you two should get along nicely, both being warriors and all."

"Raynor. I shall keep that in mind." He wandered a ways off the path, looking around until he found what he wanted. "Here," he called to her. "We'll make camp here. There's a patch of level ground where I can build a fire and we can bed down for the night."

"Oh my, are you planning on building a bed? That would be most considerate of you."

"Nay," he said slowly. "That's a way of saying there is a flat space where we can lie down and sleep."

"Oh," she sighed, "that's too bad. A bed would be nice. I could summon one if you like."

"I'm sure ye could, but I ask that ye don't. 'Tis only for one night. I'm sure ye can survive."

She shrugged off his concern. "I shall endeavor to make the best of it. But first, I suggest we eat. I find living in this world makes me hungry."

Unlike the world of the fae, earth was harsh and demanding, and he wondered how much physical labor she was willing to withstand while she was here. "Mayhap ye should make yerself useful while I go down to the loch and try to catch some fish for our supper."

29

"Are you suggesting I should sit here and wait?" She blinked up at him with a puzzled expression.

"Nay. I am suggesting ye gather some sticks and twigs, and if ye can manage, a good fallen branch or two would be nice, so I can build a fire. After that, if ye still have time, I suggest ye start clearing a space for us to sleep, someplace without rocks or tree roots to poke us in our backs. Ye might want to cover it with some moss or leaves to cushion us from the ground."

She stared up at him in disbelief. "That seems like an awful lot of work for very little results when I can simply summon a blazing fire and some soft down quilts upon which to lie."

He came to her and placed his hands on her shoulders. She seemed so frail and delicate; 'twas obvious she was not of his world. "Dear Lady Sophie, I realized we do things differently here, but that's the point. Ye are here, and it seems rather fitting ye should abide by the laws of our land. Please, doona misunderstand. I appreciate all ye have done for me. I would still be back on that beach, struggling to stay alive, if 'twas not for ye; but we humans tend to see everything as a struggle to overcome, and we usually succeed. I thank ye for all ye have done to heal my bruised and battered body, but as a man of this world, I'd like to believe I am capable of caring for yer needs. I realize ye could summon whatever we need, but that is not how it's done. I would appreciate it if we could do this the human way."

As he spoke, he watched her eyes grow large with wonder. He had the feeling no one had ever spoken to her in such a manner afore and he wondered how she would respond.

"But I've never done any of those things before. I wouldn't know how to start."

This was going to be harder than he had expected. He shook his head and sighed. "Maybe ye should come with me to the loch while I try to catch some fish. Ye can wash and get a drink of water while we're there. On the way back, we can gather fire wood together."

She continued to look at him with doe-like eyes. "No wine?"

He shook his head. "Nay, only water."

"No cheese or grapes?"

"Nay, only fish. I propose we do this the human way."

She remained silent for a while, looking off into the distance. Finally, looking less than happy, she said with a huff, "All right, I agree. I shall try."

"It will make a much better story to tell yer friends," he offered as solace. He was grateful enough to have won this battle.

That perked her up, and her smile returned. "What a good idea. It will be much more interesting to tell them I actually managed to live by your rules, primitive as they may be."

Herrick didn't care for the idea that Sophie was using her time with him as fodder for stories to entertain her fae friends back on Avalee, but accepted that for now, she had agreed to do things his way.

A couple of hours later, Herrick sat next to Sophie on a stump, enjoying the last of the fish he had caught and cooked over the fire he had built with the wood he had gathered while she had watched. Interestingly, he had managed to catch two of the biggest trout he had ever seen. They had nearly impaled themselves on the sharpened stick he had fashioned into a fishing spear. He suspected Sophie had something to do with them appearing after several uneventful minutes of watching and waiting for something to happen. Fishing, he had told her, required finesse and patience and perseverance; but it seemed the little faerie had a short rope when it came to patience.

Sophie sat back and licked her fingers. "That was better than I expected. How was I to know fresh trout cooked over an open fire could taste so good?"

"I'm glad ye liked it." He had to agree, 'twas the best meal he had enjoyed in weeks, ever since he'd gone into battle with the bloody MacDonalds. *I swear, someday that clan will be the death of me and my clansmen*, he thought morosely.

He stood and tossed the remains of his meal into the fire, gesturing for Sophie to do the same. "'Tis time for us to bed down for the night. I will walk with ye to the loch so ye may wash, or whatever ladies need do afore they go to bed." He felt the back of his neck grow hot and flushed. He had never been this uncomfortable in front of a woman afore. Although this wasn't the first time he would be bedding down with one, it might very well be the first time he would do so without the intention of taking her body for the pleasure of his.

She nodded with a laugh. It seemed she liked to laugh, a lot, and for some odd reason, that pleased him. "Yes, I think I understand," she said and linked her hand around his arm as he led her back down the darkened path to the loch. Her breast brushed up against his arm, and he wondered how long he could keep his intentions honorable.

When they returned, he began to bank the red hot coals while she sat and watched. "Ye can have the spot closest to the fire," he offered.

She stared down in disbelief. "Are we really going to lie down on the ground? With nothing to cushion us?"

"That's right, nothing but the grass and leaves Mother Nature provides. Thankfully, we also have these marvelous cloaks ye have provided to keep us warm."

Her smile was noticeably smug. "It would seem my talents are useful after all."

"Yer talents are very useful. I would be the first to agree. And I'm sure ye could spend yer time here summoning everything ye need or want, but then why be here? Why not return to Avalee where all those things are readily available?"

"Is that what you want? Do you want me to leave?" The hurt in her eyes seemed genuine.

His bluster faded. "Nay, Lady Sophie, that is not what I want," he said as humbly as he could manage. *Dang,* he liked having her around; but he didn't like it when she used her magick to summon everything she wanted, simply because she could. He wasn't comfortable being dependent on anyone for anything. Usually his family was dependent on him to survive. "This is yer adventure. Ye must choose how to proceed."

She stood and shook out her skirts. "I'll take the spot near the fire, as you suggest."

"I think 'tis best. I shall lie behind ye to break the wind and keep ye warm."

They took their places on the grassy patch of earth. She turned on her side, away from him, facing the low burning fire. After wrapping her snugly in her cloak, he turned on his back and stared up at the tops of the trees arching overhead. The stars twinkled merrily in the dark sky beyond.

What the blue blazes had he gotten himself into? And why was he so adamant against her using her powers? Probably because he knew that wasn't how things worked in his world. Life didn't come easily. It required hard work and determination. She should either agree to abide by their rules or take herself back home. No matter how many fish or quilts or warm cloaks or any other little comforts she summoned, eventually she would be gone, returned to where she came from, and he would go on living, alone in this world, without her. 'Twas best if he didn't become too accustomed to the gifts she could provide.

"Herrick," he heard her softly call."

"Aye, Lady Sophie," he answered, still looking up at the sky.

"Are you glad I'm here?"

"Aye, my lady."

"Do you want me to stay?"

How could he answer? Honestly? Aye, he wanted her to stay. "If that is what ye want," he said.

"But what do *you* want? Certainly you have a preference."

He rolled to his side, spooning her back and brought his mouth close to her ear. "I would prefer to hold ye as we sleep and wake to find ye still in my arms in the morning."

She turned her head to look up at him, her smile sweet and beckoning in the moonlight. "Thank you, Herrick. That means a lot to me."

Afore she could turn away or he could change his mind, he brought his lips down upon hers. He had never kissed a faerie afore, and he wondered how she would taste. 'Twas beyond anything he could have imagined. She tasted of exotic spices and apple pie, and smelled of fresh air and rain water. The moment their lips touched a surge of energy shot through him, heating his skin and filling him with wonder and power. Sophie rolled over to face him then wrapped her arms around his neck to hold him close as she returned his kiss with matching desire. The air around them took on a pulsating glow, dancing with every color of the rainbow. He felt as if he were being sucked into a vortex.

Just when he felt he would become lost in the bliss, she slid her hands down to his shoulders and pushed him away, breaking off the kiss.

The light in her eyes and the smile on her face were more brilliant than any he had ever seen afore.

"I should warn you," she said, sounding somewhat breathless. "We faeries are a passionate folk. I am more so than most. It may not be wise to continue down this path unless you are prepared to fully experience all I have to give, for I shall not hold back once we have begun."

He pulled back slightly to look into her eyes. They reflected the same passion and fire consuming him. "That is something to be considered," he mused as he leaned down again, ready to continue their kiss.

She held him back. "I don't think you understand, at least not yet. Perhaps it would be best to return to your original suggestion."

He stared at her blankly as the twinkling lights slowly faded afore his eyes. He had forgotten exactly what his suggestion had been.

"It would be best if you simply hold me in your arms as we sleep. It's been a rather long and eventful day. I expect we have another long day of travel ahead of us."

Blinking away the last of the dancing lights, he finally understood. She was asking him to stop. He would respect her wishes. He had never forced himself on a woman, and no matter how hotly she stirred his desires, he wouldn't do so now.

Still staring into her mesmerizing blue eyes, he gave a reluctant nod. "Agreed."

She settled in to snuggle against him as he pulled her close, wrapping his arms around her. A moment later he closed his eyes, and within seconds, he drifted off into a deep and dreamy sleep.

~~~

Sophie closed her eyes and worked to bring her thoughts and emotions back under control. It had taken a surprising amount of willpower to break off their kiss, but she had felt the energies gathering around them, energies that were set to explode into the ether, and the last thing she needed right now was to cause such a disturbance. Something like that would easily be detected by her family, especially her sister the queen. She was certain if her sisters realized where she had gone, they would send another faerie, or an elf, or even a troll to summon her back home. But she wasn't ready to return, not yet. Not when things had just become interesting.

There was no doubt in her mind that before she left this earth she would take her pleasure with Herrick. She had great plans for making love to him, but it wouldn't be on the ground in the dirt in front of a banked fire. She wondered if it should be outside under the stars or in a castle or a cottage. Regardless of where it took place, when she made love to Herrick—and she had plenty of reasons to believe she would—it would be on a silk covered bed, surrounded by plenty of plush down quilts.

She understood his concerns about using her power. As they had journeyed, she had listened to the birds, the animals, and the trees tell her of the life they lived. Still, a part of her refused to give in to the drudgery he spoke of, not when they were surrounded by so much beauty. Herrick, it seemed, had seen too much of life's harsher realities. He had become blind to the abundance this world had to offer. Now that she was here, drawn to him in ways she didn't fully understand, she saw no reason why she couldn't be the one to bring the light back into his eyes. She may have healed his sight, but there was still much he could not see. It would be her mission, she decided, that before she left, he would truly see the beauty of the world that gave him life.

Sophie wasn't quite as naïve as she acted, although she did rather enjoy watching Herrick try to school her in his ways. Perhaps she had summoned those big fat trout to come swimming their way, or maybe they were simply dazzled by her fae presence and were naturally drawn to her. Who was to say for sure? She was certainly grateful for the meal they provided and, she believed, so was Herrick. Oh, he might argue against her magic, but she had something he wanted, even if he wasn't ready to admit it quite yet. That was all right; she had time; time enough to show him the error in his ways.

For now, it was enough to experience falling asleep in his arms, feeling the weight and warmth of his body next to hers, as she happily plotted how she was going to make this all go her way.

CHAPTER 3

Herrick dreamed of greeting the dawn with Lady Sophie lying next to him, snuggled safely in his arms, but when he awoke, he found the little faerie sitting in front of him on her haunches with a finger to his lips. He opened his mouth to draw it in, but she pulled it back and waved it in his face.

"Quiet. There are men in the area. We haven't much time."

Herrick listened for signs of activity. He heard nothing. "How do ye ken?"

Sophie gave him a scathing look. "Trust me; I know. I have sent Raynor into the woods to hide. Do not disclose I am here, for they will not be able to see me."

What did she mean? Could no one else see her? For a brief second, he wondered if he had imagined her, but he quickly reminded himself the horse was real. He certainly hadn't walked from the beach to this camp.

She picked up her cloak from the ground, shook it out, and then draped it around her shoulders, only a moment afore he, too, heard the men ambling through the underbrush of the woods. Herrick jumped to his feet, grabbed his own cloak, and then tossed it under a nearby bush.

"Is that how you take care of your belongings?" she chided.

"I canna let it be seen. Men returning from battle doona carry such expensive garments."

Herrick stared at her in disbelief. Where the hell had his innocent little faerie gone? And when had she been replaced with this battle ready vixen? This certainly didn't seem like the naïve little waif who had accompanied him yesterday and fallen asleep in his arms. Not that this was a bad thing; he rather liked this bolder, stronger version of Lady Sophie.

He had no more than a minute to ready himself afore he saw the men break through the trees. Instinctively, he took a fighting stance with his right hand resting in readiness on the broadsword hanging from his belt.

A moment later, he relaxed his stance. "By jove! 'Tis Tormod MacLeod and his younger brother Harold." Herrick greeted his old friends loudly so Sophie could hear. "Ye be a sight for sore eyes, and I should ken, for I've been nearly blind for the past several days."

The two MacLeod brothers easily matched him in weight and brawn. Tormod was long, lean, and a wee taller than Herrick. Of the two brothers, Tormod was also known to do well with the lasses. Herrick figured Tormod was the type of man they could get their arms around whereas his younger brother, Harold, was not nearly as tall but twice as thick. He tended to hunch over and walked stepping side to side rather than marching forward in a straight and narrow path with one foot in front of the other. Herrick was thankful these men were friends and not foe. He hadn't the heart for another fight, but he would do whatever it took to protect Sophie and save his own life and limb.

"Well, I'll be damned, 'tis Herrick of the MacNicol clan! What brings ye to our part of the isle?" Tormod asked.

"I'm on my way home from fighting on Harris."

"Ye were on Harris with the MacDonalds?"

"Not of my choosing, I can assure ye."

"We heard there'd been a skirmish. What was it all about?"

Tormod MacLeod stepped over a large fallen tree that lay between them and took a seat. It looked as though he planned to be there awhile. Harold did the same, taking a seat beside his elder brother. Herrick figured he might as well make himself comfortable and planted his arse on a bolder a few feet away. Sophie, he noticed, remained standing with her hands on her hips and a disgruntled look upon her elfin face.

Happy for the companionship of his old friends, Herrick began to tell his tale. "'Twas another Viking raid. King Olaf the Red against Big Red of the MacDonalds and a handful of MacNicols. The Vikings figured someone had something they wanted and thought the best way to go about getting that something was with brute force. I heard one of Big Red MacDonald's daughters was kidnaped by the Vikings during one of their raids on the island and was set to marry Olaf's son. The Viking king must have thought such a union would give him rights to MacDonald's lands. Only the MacDonalds had a different idea. Olaf called in his Norse relatives to keep Big Red off their island, and the MacDonalds dragged along a few MacNicols to use as their front line." The others had included his uncle Nicail, his clan chieftain, and Nicail's two sons, Neall and Aleck. Herrick was fairly certain he had seen Neall fall in battle, but he prayed to God Uncle Nicail and Aleck were still alive and safe.

"What a blazing idiot," Tormod said, shaking his head. "That man has cabbage for brains, and the worst of it is, his clansmen will follow him into battle the minute he says go. I remember when old Big Red MacDonald threatened to take on Dunvegan. He must have sat encamped outside our castle for a good week and a half afore his arse got rained out and he dragged his sorry backside back to his own keep."

Herrick glanced over at Sophie. She had plopped herself down on a stump and sat with her elbows propped on her knees and her chin resting on her hands. From her expression, he could guess two things: she was listening to everything they said and she was bored stiff. They were swapping war stories, and this could take a while. She would have to wait and maybe learn a little patience.

He turned his attention back to the MacLeod brothers. "I ken this is yer land, or at least I must be close, but what has ye out this far and not home warm in yer beds?"

"Stupid wandering cattle, what else? Some strays were spotted up this way, and Da sent us to come and herd them home. Care to join us? We could use yer help, and ye would be welcome to stay a while once we get those cattle back home."

Herrick slipped another glance at Sophie. Shaking her head, she looked none too pleased by Tormod's suggestion. "Sorry lads. Mahap next time. After all that's happened, I need to get back home."

"I'm guessing ye are anxious to be seeing about yer Ma. How is she doing?"

"Last I saw of her, she was doing fine, but ye are right, I am in a hurry to get home." His mother tended to be home alone more often than he liked. Ever since his father died a few years back, she had insisted on living alone in their cottage while Herrick was dragged off to fight one battle or another. Nicail was his mother's brother and the clan's chief, but as far as Herrick was concerned, Nicail had not done enough to protect his sister after her husband had died. Their clan needed someone stronger to lead them. Someone who would defend the clan against the MacDonalds instead of joining them in a battle they were destined to lose. He blamed his uncle as much as Big Red for dragging him into their battle with the Vikings.

"Did yer mother not ken Big Red would come and take ye?" Tormod asked.

Herrick understood the reason for Tormod's question. He was referring to his mother's gift of second sight, her ability to see the future. Nonetheless, her visions were limited and sometimes unreliable. There were a few, like Tormod, who believed and accepted her sight as a gift of birth, but there were others who feared she had ties to the fae, or even worse, was a witch and couldn't be trusted. He dismissed those folks as being nothing more than ignorant dogs, but their prejudice had caused his mother and father to build their cottage in the hills above the village of Scorrybreac where his uncle and the rest of their clan lived.

It was only because he had been down in the village when Big Red came storming through, collecting men for his battle with the Vikings, that he had gotten caught up in the fighting. If he had been home, caring for his mother where he belonged, none of this would have happened. But a man of his years needed the companionship of others, and he had gone to Scorrybreac in search of entertainment. Instead, he had been sucked into another round of fighting. He might be good with a sword, but he had grown tired of wielding the damn thing every time someone got their nose bent out of shape.

Though he tried not to let it show, his biggest worry was whether or not his uncle and cousins had lived through the battle. He certainly hoped they had, because he didn't want to think about what it would mean if they hadn't.

"She told me not to go down to the village—said I was only looking for trouble—but I figured she was referring to the ale I was planning to drink." Herrick snuck another quick glance at Sophie to see if she caught the hint about his mother. If she did, she showed no sign of it. Her expression didn't change. She still looked bored.

"I say MacDonald should be glad someone wanted his daughter enough to take her off his hands. I wouldn't want Becca MacDonald sharing my bed night after night," Harold spoke for the first time, offering his opinion on the matter.

"I'd say she's probably in agreement with ye there as I've never seen her say so much as a fare thee well to yer ugly mug," Tormod teased, accompanying his remark with a powerful punch to his brother's arm.

"Aye, as if she's ever shown ye a bit of interest either," Harold retaliated. He leaned back to avoid the brunt of another blow from his brother then took a swing that fell shy of its mark.

"More than ye might ken. But 'tis me who has nay interest in her. She's Big Red's daughter. Olaf should have kenned he was courting disaster. I hope she was worth the trouble." Of the two brothers, Tormod was better looking and was known for having better luck with the ladies, much better luck.

"Nay woman is worth that kind of trouble," Harold said, rubbing his bruised shoulder.

Sophie, Herrick noticed, had gotten a chuckle out of the brothers' sparing.

"I've kenned a lass or two who were worth a wee bit of trouble; wouldn't ye agree, Herrick? Remember that night with the Monroe sisters? They had quite a taste for dick'en cider," Tormod said with a wolfish grin. He then went into a fair amount of detail, recalling what had happened and how both of the sisters had eventually ended up in his bed.

45

Tormod accentuated his tale by scratching his ballocks with an obvious adjustment to his man parts. "Wasn't that a night o' fun?"

Sophie's eyes jerked to meet Herrick's, as though she were intently awaiting his response.

Herrick couldn't hold back the chuckles her reaction provoked. "Aye, Tormod, we've had our fair share of fun with the lovely lasses."

"We've got to get our cows back to pasture, but later this eve we hope to visit the village. If ye can spare the time, ye would be welcome to join us," Tormod went on. "I heard Katie has been making visits to the Boar's Head Pub. I'm sure she'd be right happy to see yer arse again."

Herrick sneaked a peek at Sophie. She didn't look happy. Suddenly, she was on her feet, waving her slender hand at the men sitting across from him. Herrick hoped she wasn't casting some type of spell over their manly parts, or his either for that matter.

A startled look came over Harold and Tormod. They each gave their head a little shake, and together they stood.

"We've lingered long enough," Tormod said, looking a little dazed. "'Tis time for us to get back to rounding up those cattle."

Herrick wondered what had just happened. He stood also. "Aye, and 'tis time I continued my journey home. Be sure to send word to me next time the MacLeod's are hosting a gathering, mayhap for yer union with Lacie. I'd welcome the opportunity to drink to yer health."

"So we shall, my friend, so we shall. Now 'tis best we all be on our way. Fare thee well on yer journey home."

"I'll do my best," Herrick said with a grin. He cast a glance at Sophie. She looked as angry as a stirred up hornets' nest. 'Twas obvious she had become disenchanted with their talk and was anxious to have the MacLeod brothers hurry on their way.

When the men were out of hearing, Herrick turned to face her. "Lady Sophie-e-e," he said, drawing out her name. "What did ye do to those two men?"

"Not nearly as much as I wanted. I simply reminded them they had a job to do and it didn't include sitting here with you talking about their female encounters." She sounded about as mad as she looked.

"No spells upon their manhood?" He watched her through narrowed eyes.

"No!" She sneered in disgust. "Although, perhaps if I had thought of it, it wouldn't have been a bad idea. Especially for that bigger one. He seemed awfully sure of himself."

"Tormod has quite a history with the ladies, but he's betrothed to Lacie Ewart, and I'm thinking he'll be settling down sometime soon."

"I pity the poor woman. That man is not to be trusted."

"Wait just a minute here. Dinna ye tell me, just last night, the fae are a passionate people, and ye more so than most? That type of statement leads me to believe ye are not without experiences of yer own. How else could ye state such a thing? What would an innocent ken of passion?"

"I never claimed to be innocent, and that's not what we're talking about here. I can tell from his thoughts and words, that man did not give pleasure; he took it. It was a falsehood to let those women believe he cared for them or their wellbeing. The way he described them and their actions shows a lack of respect. It was as if he, as a man, had the right to enjoy the pleasures of lust, but those women are somehow less than him if they also enjoyed it. Is my observation not correct?"

Herrick stared at her in stony silence, wondering how he should respond to her emotional outburst. Not surprisingly, she didn't give him a chance to say a word afore she continued on with her rant.

"No fae male would ever abuse the respect of a fae female. Every act of passion is appreciated and reciprocated or it does not take place. We may share our passions more freely than you lowly humans, but we do not flaunt our encounters as if they were victories won over another. Do I make myself clear?"

Herrick's anger smoldered just below the surface, but he kept it in check. "I believe ye do, Lady Sophie."

She took a deep breath and smoothed out her skirts. "Now then, I forgive you for your actions of the past. They are behind us, so we shall not linger on such thoughts."

His eyes went wide. "Excuse me? Ye forgive me? I've done nothing that requires yer forgiveness."

"It's your disrespect toward women I am forgiving."

"I have never in my life intentionally disrespected a woman."

"Can you honestly say you have never engaged in such crass tales as your friend just did, using the actions of a woman to make yourself look stronger, better, more deserving?"

Herrick had to think about that. It wasn't uncommon for men to sit around drinking and telling tall tales of their sexual prowess; he was sure he had done his fair share at one time or another. But what did it matter? It was only done in the company of other men.

As if she had read his thoughts, she continued, "Whenever men take part in these sharing of tales, they show their disrespect toward women and their acceptance, even their approval, of such actions. And that perpetuates the acceptance and approval onto other men, and the cycle continues without end. This is why there is so little hope for your race. Men will always fight, and fornicate, and show disrespect to their fellow humans. It was a silly, foolish, crazy idea to come and visit this land. My sisters are right. Humans are not worth the time."

"Now wait just a minute there, little lassie. I dinna invite ye here, and while I appreciate everything ye have done for me, not once have I been disrespectful or acted in an unkind manner. It seems to me ye are judging all of humankind based on one man's actions. And I doona think what he did was even that bad."

"That's exactly my point."

"It would be different if we were talking about Big Red MacDonald. That man is a scourge on the face of mankind, but Tormod is a good man. He does his duty by his family and his clan, and he shouldn't be condemned for a bit of boasting about a night of fun where no one was hurt. Isn't that why ye came here, to have yer bit of fun? Mahap now ye can go back to yer friends in Avalee and tell them yer story of how ye made fun of us humans and put us in our place. How would that be any different from what Tormod did? How would *ye* be any different? Wouldn't yer story serve to make ye look stronger, better, and more deserving? As far as I can tell, ye are no different than us."

"How dare you?" Her arms wrapped around her middle as if she needed to contain herself.

"What? Tell ye the truth? Or is that concept reserved only for the fae?"

"I told you, I am a person of passion." Her anger was riding high, and it showed in the tone of her voice. "When I'm mad, I get very mad. When I'm happy, I am very happy, and when I . . ." She stopped herself afore she said what she was thinking and turned her back on him. "And right now I am not very happy." Several seconds ticked by in awkward silence afore she spoke again. When she did, her voice was softer, even a bit misty. "It's not fun to have my faults pointed out to me. I hope you will not make a habit of that."

Dang, the woman had a way of turning his insides into knots until he dinna ken if he were coming or going. He really should take off and leave her behind, but there wasn't a bone in his body that would let him walk away from her.

His anger dissipated, and in its place was something new: compassion. "This is simply what people do when they care for each other. They tell them what they think and how they feel."

She kept her back turned towards him. "I never said I care about you."

"I've always believed actions speak louder than words. Yer actions tell me ye care, even if only a little. Ye care enough to want me to be better."

She turned to face him. "Your actions speak loudly, as well. You are a good man, Herrick of the MacNicols. For a traveling companion, I have chosen well."

He bowed to her with respect. "I am honored."

"I think it's time for Raynor to return and we continue on our journey. Have you any suggestions for breakfast, or must we eat fish again?"

He smiled and shook his head with a sigh of relief. There was one thing he could say about Lady Sophie: he had no doubt she would keep him on his toes. "As a show of respect, I shall leave it up to ye. I'll nay longer fight ye for being who ye are."

Sophie gazed at him for a long moment with appreciative eyes. "A little birdie told me there is a croft not far from here. Perhaps the people who live there will be so good as to share a couple of eggs and a slice of bread with us. If we are truly lucky, they may even have some cheese and ale."

Herrick stepped closer to her, wanting to close the gap between them. "And how would we repay such generosity?" he wondered.

She turned to retrieve his cloak from beneath the bush where he had flung it then walked up to him. "Perhaps they would like one of these warm and expensive looking cloaks," she said, smiling.

Herrick was glad, he liked to see her smile. He nodded and said, "I will gladly give up mine so we may eat."

"Your gesture is appreciated," Sophie said. "But it won't be necessary. I happen to know there is always more where this came from." She gently shook the leaves and dirt from the cloak and handed it to Herrick.

Herrick's hand brushed Sophie's as he accepted the plush garment, and he met her gaze once more.

"Ah," she said, breaking the momentary silence. "Here is Raynor now. Let us be on our way."

He took a step back to bow. "As ye wish, Lady Sophie."

CHAPTER 4

As Raynor carried them down the road, Herrick replayed his time with Sophie in his head, wondering if there was any possible way he could figure her out. The task was probably hopeless, but at least it kept his mind busy and his thoughts away from focusing solely on the pleasurable feeling of her soft, warm, supple body sitting so close to his. She was right in that regard. When it came to women, men's minds tended to be consumed with thoughts of lust.

When he first met the little faerie, she seemed naïve and innocent to the point of being child-like. By nightfall, she had demonstrated she was a woman of passion and had hinted of pleasures she had yet to give when the time was right. He rather liked the idea she might share her mystical body with him and could honestly admit he would welcome the opportunity to experience making love with a faerie such as her.

This morning, she had shown she was fiercely protective by the way she had warned him of men in the area, and what she feared was approaching danger. She was also extremely opinionated and emotional. It occurred to him that keeping track of Sophie's moods was not going to be easy. If anything, it would be a challenge. The best challenge he'd had in a long, long time.

"Look there," she said, bringing his thoughts back to the present. "That must be the croft the little birdie spoke of. A small white dwelling where people live and work the land, am I not right?"

Herrick looked down to see her expression of wide-eyed wonder. Naïve Sophie had reappeared. "Aye, that is a croft," he said.

Smoke rose from the chimney and there were signs of activity about the place. A handful of chickens roamed freely in the yard. Without another word from him, the horse walked up to the lane in front of the cottage and stopped. Herrick wondered if a horse such as this would perform as well in combat, but then quickly remembered he had vowed to forsake all future battles.

Herrick dismounted and helped Sophie to the ground. She took a moment to straighten her skirts and fluff her cloak. As she preened, she seemed to become refreshed and even lovelier, if such a thing were possible.

"I am anxious to meet these new people," she said as she prepared herself. "Do you think they will like me?"

Herrick looked her over with appreciative eyes. "They will think ye are royalty and I am but yer humble servant to escort ye along yer way. I would be surprised if they are not anxious to share their best with ye."

"Really? Do you really think they will take me for royalty?" she asked, looking pleased.

"Look how ye are dressed. Yer garments are finely made with expensive cloth. Ye ride upon a mighty steed, albeit one without a saddle. No one would think ye a poor little peasant lass."

"Oh, you're right. I don't want to stand out. I should appear as one of your own. Let me know if this is not better." With a wave of her hand, her garments became plain and simple versions of what they had been only seconds afore. Her diaphanous blue silken gown became a dull grey dress, and her cloak appeared to be made from rough, work-a-day wool instead of finely woven fabric and luxurious fur.

"Aye, I believe that will do just fine. But nothing, my dear Lady Sophie, can disguise yer sweet and lovely face." Herrick leaned down and kissed her gently on the lips. 'Twas only meant as a sign of affection and appreciation, but when he looked into her eyes, he saw a tear ready to spill.

"Oh, Herrick, you are so very good to me." Turning to stand beside him, she linked her arm in his and said, "I believe we must have a story, shouldn't we? We can't very well say I am a faerie who appeared to you from out of the mists to heal your bruised and broken body. Should I be your sister? Your wife?" With a mischievous glint in her eyes, she looked up at him and added, "Or your lover?"

Her enthusiasm nearly caused him to choke. He cleared his throat and said, "This is but a small isle. We canna say ye are my sister, as I doona have a sister." He paused a short moment afore he added, "And while I had a wife, she has been dead for many years."

"Oh, Herrick." Sophie's eyes grew large and soulful. "You didn't tell me you had a wife."

"And a son." He looked away. "But 'tis not a tale for now."

"I am sorry for your loss."

Herrick nodded curtly. "Yer sympathy is appreciated." He cleared his throat again and forced himself to dispel the emotions he preferred to keep locked under control. When he turned to look at her again, he noticed her eyes were misty once more.

"I think 'tis best if we say I am returning from Harris," he continued, "which I am, and I am escorting ye back to yer family on the mainland. We can say ye are Lady Sophie of the Campbells of Loch Awe if we are asked."

Her eyes brightened. "Lady Sophie of the Campbells of Loch Awe. I rather like it, and it still sounds impressive."

"I doona believe anyone could see ye as less than impressive, my dear Lady Sophie."

"Oh, dear. Perhaps you shouldn't call me Lady Sophie if I am merely another peasant girl." She brought a finger up to her chin. "Umm, I think Miss Sophie will do, for now," she stated with a mocking grin.

"Mistress Campbell would be more correct," Herrick informed her.

"All right, but you must call me Mistress *Sophie* Campbell. If you do not refer to me as Sophie, I may not know who you are speaking to."

"As ye wish."

As they approached the cottage, a young lad came running out from behind an outbuilding. "Ma, Ma, we have visitors. They've come riding on a big grey horse. Ma, Ma, come look."

Herrick glanced at Sophie. "It appears they doona have visitors here very often."

"Is that a good thing, or a bad thing?" she asked.

Herrick shrugged. "We shall see." The Highlanders of Skye were known for their rule of hospitality to any and all who visited their homes. He expected it wouldn't be any different at this cottage. The dwelling and its occupants appeared poor, but no poorer than most on the island.

A woman of middle years, dressed in some of the finest homespun he had ever seen, came to the door in response to her son's calling. "Travis Duffie, is that anyway to announce our guests? The way ye be shouting, ye would think the King of bloody England had come to call." When she spied Herrick and Sophie, she wiped her hands on the stained apron covering her dress and called out to greet them. "Greetings. How may I be of service?" She looked to be not much older than Herrick, but the years weighed heavy on her well-rounded frame.

"We are travelers along this road and are in need of a wee breakfast. I am Herrick of the MacNicols, and this is Mistress Sophie of the Campbells of Loch Awe."

Sophie spoke to him under her breath. "You did that very well. It sounded very official."

Herrick did his best to not get puffed up with pride by her compliment, but the acknowledgement felt good.

"Herrick of the MacNicols! Ye must be Mable's son," the woman from the cottage greeted him in delight.

"That is correct. Do ye ken my mother?"

"We have met in years gone by when ye were only a wee lad. Welcome, welcome, come right in. I've not much I can offer, but a visitor is always welcome. Come, tell me what news there is of the world."

For many of the lonely crofters who lived and worked in the remote areas of the isle, a visitor with news to share was considered a welcomed break from the dreariness of their daily lives.

When they reached the door, she stepped aside, allowing them to pass. The interior of the cottage appeared well lived-in and suffered from hard use, but it was clean and for the most part, tidy. The front room of the cottage held a table with chairs and a bench.

"I'm Mary Duffie, and these are my children," she chirped with a flourish of motion as she swept into the room behind them.

Travis, the lad from the front yard, had joined three other children, all lasses, in the back half of the house, which was divided in two with the sleeping cots on one side and the kitchen for cooking on the other. The children appeared to range in age from the youngest being no more than a toddler up to the oldest, whom Herrick guessed to be on her way to thirteen summers. Travis seemed to fall somewhere in the middle.

Tucked into the far corner of the cottage near an open window were the tools of the trade for a weaver, a spinning wheel and a loom. The eldest daughter sat at the loom, working on a piece that, to Herrick's untrained eye, looked strangely unusual. 'Twas woven from what looked like a mismatched collection of threads and yarns of various colors and thicknesses.

"My eldest son and his da are out shepherding our sheep," Mistress Duffie continued.

Sophie appeared totally unconcerned with what Mistress Duffie was saying. Instead, in seeming rapt fascination, she made her way over to the young lass working the loom.

"Whatever is she doing?" Sophie said, watching the lass with a look of wonder.

Mistress Duffie turned to see what had caught Sophie's attention. "Why, she's weaving, of course. But I understand yer question. The piece is quite unusual. Ellie is still an apprentice. She's learning a new technique, so I thought it best if she used bits and pieces of leftover yarn from other projects and some of the wool that dinna take the dyes as well as I would have liked. This way, if she makes mistakes, we'll not be wasting our good yarn. We'll use it as an extra blanket for one of our beds."

"This is the most beautiful, wondrous piece I have ever seen. So many vibrant colors, each unique and specially woven all together. It's like a tapestry of life; up close it appears crazy and chaotic, but in its whole is beauty. Please, please, tell me you will sell it to me when she is done."

Sophie looked to Herrick with big doe-like eyes. "You'll purchase this for me, won't you Herrick?"

Herrick eyed the piece and wondered at how she could possibly view it as such. Her imagination must be grand indeed.

"Oh no, Mistress Campbell, ye canna mean to buy this. 'Tis only a child's learning piece," Mistress Duffie said, looking slightly ill at ease.

"Even if Mistress Duffie wished to part with the piece, I have no coin with which to pay," Herrick reminded her.

Sophie gave him a severe look. "I can get you the coin you need, as I'm sure you know. You can come back here, later, when she has finished, and get this as a 'boon' to me. Isn't that what you called it when you asked for my help?" She was no doubt referring to the wish she had granted him when she found him on the beach.

"Mistress Duffie has expressed she nay wishes to sell the piece." Herrick returned her glare with one of his own.

Sophie's expression turned soft and sweet, and her voice dripped with honey. "Mistress Duffie, to me this is a work of art, special and one of a kind, never to exist again. Please, I know I ask for much, but if you can find it in your heart to part with it, I will gladly pay whatever you ask."

Mistress Duffie looked stunned. "Oh, Lordy child, that isn't necessary. I'll send word to Mable when 'tis finished, and Herrick can come back and fetch it. 'Twould be an extra blessing to me if yer dear sweet mother could accompany ye on the journey. 'Tis been ages since we've been able to have a good visit and chat the day away. That will be payment enough, I assure ye."

Herrick looked at the two women afore him. He was caught. There seemed no good way to deny either one of them. It looked as though he would be coming back this way sometime soon and bringing his mother with him. There was still one piece of the puzzle that bothered him; he hadn't expected Sophie to stay around much longer. How did she hope to collect this particular piece of fabric when it was finished, and what would she need with a child's unskilled and coarse mishmash blanket? To him, it looked like a jumble of yarns and colors, and yet Sophie saw it as beautiful. Once again, the faerie's thoughts were beyond his comprehension.

Reluctantly, Herrick accepted defeat. "It appears as though my mother and I will be paying ye another visit, Mistress Duffie."

The woman seemed thoroughly delighted and was suddenly alight with activity. "'Tis grand. Now, come sit down to break yer fast. I've not much, but what I have, ye are welcome to share. I can offer ye an egg or two and a thick slice of fresh baked bread with butter and a mug of ale."

Sophie surprised Herrick by saying, "It sounds like a feast. We are most grateful. I wish we had some way to repay you."

"Tell me the news from whence ye come and where ye are going, and that shall be payment enough. How is yer dear, saintly mother, Herrick?"

Sophie exchanged a glance with Herrick as they took seats across from each other at the table. He nodded, not completely happy with her, but still hoped to put her at ease.

"She is well, last I ken. I have been off fighting with the MacDonalds against a Viking raid on the Isle of Harris and am returning home. Along the way, I was asked to escort Mistress Sophie of the Campbells back home," Herrick informed their hostess.

"Is Big Red at it again? I swear to the saints above, that man and his kin are more trouble than they are worth. I be guessing he rounded up ye and yer kinsmen and kindly persuaded ye to join him in his battle."

"Aye, ye would be right, although I wouldna say it was so kindly."

"'Tis his way," she said with a weary shake of her head. "Someday 'twill be different, but that's a long way coming. Let me fry up those eggs as we speak." She went over to the kitchen cupboard and pulled out a wooden bowl. "Well, glory be. I thought we only had two left, but there's half a dozen in here now." She looked to her eldest daughter. "Did ye gather more eggs than usual this morning?"

"Nay, Ma. I showed ye all the eggs I brought in," Ellie answered shyly with hardly a glance from her work at the loom. All the earlier attention seemed to have frightened the young lass.

"Well, never mind. I must have miscounted," Mistress Duffie said with a look of disbelief.

Herrick glanced quickly at Sophie; she responded with the slightest of shrugs.

Mary took the large iron skillet resting near the hearth and placed it over the fire. While she waited for it to heat, she pulled out a loaf of bread and cut off two thick slices; Herrick could smell the fresh baked aroma.

"So tell me, Mistress Campbell," Mary said, "why is a pretty young lass such as yerself so far from home?"

Herrick began to speak, but Sophie rushed to answer. "I was sent by my father to be betrothed to Kyle of the MacNeils on the Isle of Harris, but he was lost in the battle with the Vikings. Herrick of the MacNicols was kind enough to take on the task of taking me back to my family," she said dramatically. Sophie looked to Herrick, batting her eyes with a devilishly mischievous grin, but he could only roll his eyes with a shake of his head. Lady Sophie was playing her role well. "I don't know what I would have done without him."

"How dreadful," Mary said.

"No, not at all. I've never met Kyle, so his death was no great loss, at least not to me. Although I am sure his family grieves. I have been told he was most fair to gaze upon, but surely not as fair and brawn as Herrick, who survived the battle. So you see, I am most fortunate to have Herrick as my escort. He has proven to be most able. Last night, he caught two of the biggest trout I have ever seen and cooked them up pretty as you please. I thought I was eating like a faerie princess, it tasted so good."

Herrick gave her a knowing glance as he nudged her under the table. "Putting it on a bit thick," he teased softly, but he couldn't help but smile. So she found him fair and brawn, did she? That was nice to ken. Seeing Sophie enjoying herself, it was hard to not share her good spirits.

Herrick noticed the toddler had waddled her way over to Sophie and was pulling herself up by Sophie's skirts. "Faerie . . . princess," she cooed in awe.

"Bella, doona be bothering our guests," Mary said, stooping to pick up the child.

"Faerie, princess," Bella cooed again.

Herrick watched Sophie's reaction, wondering if she was concerned by the child's prattle, but she gave no indication it was anything more than a baby's jabbering.

"Really, she's no bother," Sophie assured the mother. She pulled the child into her lap. "Well hello, sweetie, what have you got there?" she asked, pointing to the wooden toy held tightly in the child's hand. "Is that a little horse?" Sophie began to play with the child's toy, galloping it up and down the table in front of her, making the child laugh with glee.

Apparently convinced her youngest daughter wasn't a bother to her guest, Mistress Duffie went back to her work, preparing their simple meal. "Herrick is a good man," Mary went on to say, keeping an eye on her youngest. "From what I ken of yer ma, I'd expect nothing less, such a fine woman she is. Dinna I hear ye got married a while back? To Lolanie of Clan Donald? And ye had a son, Rory," Mary chatted away, but as she was speaking, it became evident to Herrick she regretted her words. "Forgive me, Herrick, I dinna ken." She glanced nervously at Sophie afore adding, "I must have forgotten about the loss of yer wife and son. 'Twas the MacDonald of Sleat, as I recall."

Much like his mother, Herrick realized Mistress Duffie had the gift of seeing. It helped to explain why she and her family would be living so far from the community of a village. Women with the sight were often mistrusted, feared, or even shunned.

"Aye, but it has been a while. I can understand yer forgetting. Most days I prefer not to dwell on it myself. Life goes on for the living, but 'tis not always easy." For a moment, Sophie caught his eye, but he looked away, and she returned her attention to the babe in her arms. He wasn't interested in sharing his thoughts or feelings on this subject with her, at least not yet, maybe never.

"Dreadful, I tell ye. Every one of those MacDonalds are dreadful." Mistress Duffie shook her head in disgust as she poured them each a cup of ale. The eggs were done cooking, so she served them along with the freshly cut bread on a trencher and set it in front of Sophie and Herrick. "Eat now; doona be shy. We've kept ye long enough. I'm sure ye'll be wanting to get back on the road. Ye still have two days ride to reach Portree."

After setting the toddler on the bench beside her, Sophie looked into the eyes of their hostess and offered her sincere thanks. "Thank you, Mistress Duffie. We are blessed by your generosity and loving spirit. Your children are full of beauty and light. May the stars above watch over you every day of your life."

Mary looked about to weep, she was so touched by Sophie's blessing. "Ye are most welcome, Mistress Campbell. May the stars guide ye on yer way."

As they ate, Herrick told Mary about seeing the MacLeod brothers on the road and that Tormod was betrothed to Lacie Ewart. They exchanged several other stories about people they each knew, and by the time they were ready to leave, Herrick had had his fill of food for both body and soul.

~~~

Sophie watched Herrick as he interacted with Mary Duffie and her family. She saw the respect he showed her by doing his best to protect Mary's secret. Like his mother, Mistress Duffie also had the gift of second sight. Sophie had known almost immediately when she met their hostess that she had been touched by the fae. For a moment, she worried Mary had seen through her disguise, but if she had, she too respected Sophie's secret.

The girl child, Bella, was another matter. It was obvious the babe had known who, or at least what, she was, but that hadn't surprised Sophie. The young ones were often more open to the world of the supernatural and could easily see what adults could not.

She also learned quite a bit more about Herrick, and everything she heard endeared him more to her heart. Her adventure was truly becoming dangerous. Sophie had heard stories of fae who fell in love with a human and it rarely turned out well. The fae were a long-lived race—at nearly two-hundred years, she was considered young and immature—while the humans grew old by the time they were fifty. Earthly life was hard and harsh. It took the life out of even the most hale and heartiest of men. Herrick would be no different.

He was in the prime of his life, being all of thirty summers, but his youth was behind him, and the years ahead would not be easy or kind. Sophie knew better, but still, she worried for him. And for herself, for the feelings she would take with her when she returned to Avalee.

"I'm stuffed," Herrick said when they were back on the road. "I've not eaten this well since I left my mother's house. That was very kind of ye to gift them with extra eggs."

"I left them with more than eggs. I gave them the blessing of the fae. For their kindness to strangers, they shall never know lack for the rest of their days. It will not be much, not much more than enough, but their chickens will lay eggs and their sheep will be fertile and wooly. Acts of kindness should always be rewarded," Sophie told him.

"On behalf of the Duffies, I thank ye."

"You and the Duffies are most welcome. And don't you forget, you and your mother will be back here soon to collect my fabric from little Ellie. I know that will mean so much to Mistress Mary Duffie. So what comes next, Herrick of the MacNicols? Now that our bellies are full, what adventures await us this day?"

"With ye, Lady Sophie, one can only guess."

After reaching the lower tip of Loch Dunvegan, Herrick took the road heading east across the island. He wondered if Sophie would insist on summoning cheese, wine, and grapes for their dinner as she had wanted last eve. More and more, he questioned how much he should accept from her faerie powers or how strongly he should fight against it. Gifts such as hers could make a man grow soft, and life on Skye was too harsh to tolerate soft men.

"Stop, we need to stop." They had just come over the crest of a small hill when Sophie cried out. "I want to explore that meadow." She pointed to the verdant landscape spread out before them. Tiny purple and yellow wildflowers dotted the ground. A stream ran through the middle of the meadow with runoff from the seemingly never ending rain, snow, or mists that fed the land.

Raynor stopped as ordered in the middle of the road, and Sophie leapt from the horse, landing gracefully on her feet.

"Well done," Herrick said, impressed. "Ye are as graceful as a bird in flight."

"Thank you." Sophie curtsied. "I simply imagine myself to be graceful, and I am."

"I see, rather like that imaginative story ye told back at the cottage." He dismounted easily but dropped to the ground with much less finesse.

Sophie twirled and danced, lifting her arms in sinuous movements. "Imagination is a gift; one should always put it to good use. Come, dance with me."

Herrick chuckled, shaking his head. "I doona imagine I can."

"That's the point," Sophie said. She stopped dancing to stand and face him. "You imagine yourself to be clumsy and so you are."

"I dinna say I was clumsy. Not everyone can dance with ease and grace. I've spent my life learning how to move quickly, wield a sword, and fight well. There was no time for dancing."

"You could if you wanted to, but as you've said, you cannot imagine yourself moving in such a manner, and so you can't. Your image of who you are and how you can, or cannot move, is too well established to change so quickly. But come, we have a meadow to explore."

She spread her arms wide then grabbed his hand and ran down the hillside, pulling him after her. Together they tumbled to the ground, rolling round and round down the soft green grass covering the hill until they came to rest at the bottom. As they tumbled, Sophie laughed with a sound of joy. Taking great pleasure in her happiness, Herrick laughed along with her. Only Sophie could so thoroughly enjoy something as simple as dancing or rolling through a meadow.

Sophie scrambled over to the running stream and took a long cool drink of the water. Herrick did the same.

"The nectar of the gods," Herrick said after drinking his fill.

"It's nothing more than water; fresh and refreshing to be sure, but this is hardly nectar of the gods. I should know," Sophie replied, licking her lips.

The sight of the wee pink tip gliding smoothly over her rosy lips was nearly enough for Herrick to forget his thoughts. When he realized he was staring, he forced his eyes from her lips and recalled what he had wanted to say. "The Isle of Skye is kenned for its rainfall and the year around damp, but without the blessing of rain from above, we would have nothing to drink, our crops wouldn't grow, our livestock would go thirsty. Without water, there would be no wine, no ale, no whisky. 'Tis because we have an abundance of rain on Skye that we are so blessed."

"You have an abundance of cold," Sophie said, drawing her cloak around her. "I prefer to bask in the sun while it shines." She walked over to a grass covered spot and lay down with her face turned to the sun.

Following her lead, Herrick lay down beside her.

As they rested on their backs, looking up at the sky, Sophie asked, "What did you do as a child? What was it like to be a human child?"

Herrick raised his hand to shield his eyes from a burst of sunlight streaming through the white, fluffy clouds overhead. "I did my chores, played with the other lads, and I trained."

"Trained for what?"

"I trained to be a man, to defend my family and my kinsmen. I trained to fight for my clan and protect our lands. I trained to be a warrior."

Sophie rolled on her side to face him and ran her hand lazily up and down his chest. "Did you always know you would someday be a warrior?"

"I have known nothing else."

Her hand continued its languid trail up and down his chest. He tried very hard not to become overly aroused and respond to the wanton desire she sparked in him. It wasn't easy. He kept his gaze focused on the sky above, nonetheless he could feel every touch of her fingers as they traced their way up and down his chest, dipping lower, and lower towards the belt of his plaid. When it seemed she was about to slip her long, slender fingers beneath the woolen fabric, he reached out and grabbed her hand.

Turning his head to meet her gaze, he said, "Much more of that lassie, and fae or not, I'll have ye splayed on yer back faster than ye can blink. And this time, I shall not yield."

She returned his gaze with a lazy smile. "Mmm, I'll keep that in mind." Slowly, she pulled her hand from his grasp and returned it to her side. She lay there in silence for several minutes looking up at the sky, and Herrick thought maybe she was done with her questions for the while.

She was lovely to watch. Herrick believed he could look at her all day long and never grow weary. He wondered if it was because of her unearthly beauty or if the mere presence of a faerie was more than his senses could resist. Either way, he felt compelled to keep watch over her. He forced himself to look away and turned his gaze, like hers, back to the crystal blue, cloud-laden sky.

~~~

There was something Sophie had wanted to ask Herrick about since their first night together, and she pondered if now were a good time. She wondered how much he would tell her or if he would tell her anything at all. Up until now she had respected his privacy in the matter, but her patience had its limits.

"Will you tell me about your wife and son?" she asked, her voice low and soft.

Still gazing at the sky, she felt the muscles of his body tense beside her. She reached over to grasp his hand and waited. For a long moment, he did not speak.

"Lolanie needed a husband, and I needed a wife," he eventually said, his voice strangely flat.

She turned to see his face. It appeared to be chiseled out of rock. "Did you not love her?"

His gaze remained skyward. "I cared for her. Aye, I loved her. We were childhood friends."

"Did she not make you a good wife? You had a son together." She wondered why this was so hard for him to talk about.

Herrick plucked a blade of grass and twisted it between his fingers. "Lolanie was of the clan Donald. She was like one of those women ye heard Tormod speak of, someone who had been sought out for a night of fun, except this was against her wishes. Lolanie hadn't been asked, and she certainly hadn't agreed. She was abused and then abandoned. She needed a protector and a husband, I needed a wife. I took her into my home, and together we raised our son."

She saw in his eyes a troubled, haunted look, as if he were searching for an answer to a question he had never dared to ask. "Did you ever think the boy may not be your own?" she asked gently.

"Nay. I chose not to think about it. The babe needed a father. He was innocent of anything that came afore him. He was my son."

Sophie doubted there were many men who would be so kind or loving. "How did you lose them?"

Again, another long pause afore he spoke. "I failed to protect them. They were traveling by boat to a nearby isle with her father, Ewan of the Donald clan. I never liked him. Dinna trust him. He failed to protect her, failed to care for her because she was a woman and not the son he had wanted. 'Tis said he was taking her and our son to the MacDonald of Sleat. I can only guess why. Their boat was hit by a harsh, sudden storm, and she was spared whatever fate he might have wished for her. If the storm hadn't killed him, I would have."

"I am truly sorry for your loss," Sophie said, still holding his hand. It was too astonishing for her to understand. These people truly were cruel and beyond redemption. Why on earth did Adam find them so fascinating? Why did he leave Avalee time and again to engage with these humans? Did he actually enjoy watching them hurt and kill each other? These people claimed they believed in an almighty God, and yet they had no love for each other.

Suddenly sorry she had pursued the subject, she rolled away and gathered some wild flowers growing nearby then began weaving them into a chain. "You said you played as a child. What did you do when you played?"

~~~

Herrick willed himself to relax, grateful to leave the subject of his family behind. She had asked, and he had answered as best he could. He appreciated that she didn't press for more. Ewan was not the only one to blame. He had left Lolanie and Rory alone while he was off fighting in another bloody skirmish with those damn McNiels of Harris. Never one to miss a battle, that time he had gone willingly. When he returned, he learned his wife and child were dead, lost to the sea at the hands of her own father. Shutting the darkness back up in its box, he focused on Sophie's question about his childhood, a much happier time.

"We played at training; we knocked wooden swords around. Or we'd hide from each other, waiting to be found. Or we explored. As a lad, I loved to roam the countryside for the mere joy of seeing what was on the other side of the crest. Ma liked to say that someday I would be a great explorer, but I've not gone far from Skye; 'tis my home. Instead, I've traveled over every inch of this isle. I've fished from the lochs, I've roamed the woods, and I've climbed the rocky Black Cuillin Mountains that rise up like jagged teeth bursting from the ground."

"You love it here, don't you?" She pulled a tiny purple wildflower from the ground and stuck it in her hair. The petals fluffed gently in the breeze.

"I canna imagine living anywhere else."

"But you have nowhere else to compare. If only you could visit Avalee. It's always warm there; never cold and damp as it is here. We have miles of sunny beaches, beautiful oceans, lush gardens, and an abundance of fragrant flowers. I would take you there, if I could, but that is not allowed. I know of no human who has ever been granted access to Avalee."

"I have heard of places such as ye speak, in the south of France and even further south to the Mediterranean Sea, but I've no need to see such places. Skye is my home, where I shall live my life and die."

"But why? Why must you be confined to this cold and remote island? You have no idea how big and wide this earth of yours is."

"Because 'tis my home. Because I am my mother's son and my uncle's nephew and have sworn my loyalty to my clan. What is a man without his clan? What place can he call his own if he wanders the earth in search of pleasures when he is needed at home?"

Sophie huffed, apparently displeased by his answer. "I don't know why I picked the Isle of Skye to visit, although I'm sure it has something to do with the layer of magic that blankets this land. I've felt it since I first arrived. The energy of the fae runs strong on this isle. I wonder why?"

"'Tis said the people of Skye have long believed in the faerie folk and the blessings or curses they bestow on the land. I think the fae appreciate our belief in them. For the most part, we are a God-fearing Christian folk, but everyone agrees, we doona mess with the fae."

Her smile turned wickedly mischievous. "Why is that? Why do we invoke such fear? As you can see for yourself, I am only a petite, little woman; surely I am no match for your strength."

"I believe I have seen only a small portion of what ye can do. We have no power against a people who can summon whatever they want and be seen or not seen as they choose. Ye are like smoke and mists, impossible to catch, or capture, or control." Their only saving grace, Herrick told himself, was the unbreakable pact that had been negotiated between the Tuatha de Danann and the ancient humans of earth. After centuries of fighting, it was agreed the fae shall never again take the life of a human nor intentionally spill their blood. But that didn't protect the humans from all the harm the fae were capable of wielding should they choose to bring blight upon the earth.

"You are wrong. I cannot summon whatever I want," Sophie said.

"But I've seen . . ."

"You've seen very little. I can only summon from what is around me. There is a horse left to pasture, so I can summon it to my side. There are sheep in the fields, so I can summon a beautifully woven wool cloak made from their fleece. I can summon nature to do my bidding, but only because I respect nature in return. Should I disregard its bounty and beauty, it would turn against me as strongly as it does you humans."

Herrick became indignant. "We doona disrespect the land. The land is the most valuable thing we own."

"You cannot *own* the land. When you fight over rights to live and work the land, is that not an act of disrespect? When you spill your neighbors' blood upon the ground, is that not an act of disrespect?"

Sophie rolled away from him and leapt to her feet. *Dang,* the woman was fast, as nimble as a sparrow in flight.

"I will not argue with you about things you do not understand." She shook out her skirts and turned away.

Herrick stood also. "Enough. We must go. We have lingered here long enough."

"What's your sudden hurry? What if I like lying here in this meadow, enjoying the sun warming my skin?" She sat back down on the grass and continued to pluck wildflowers to weave into her chain.

Herrick looked at her and shook his head. *So this is how she wants to play.* She claimed the fae didn't fight battles. Instead, she waged smaller tests of willpower, hers against his. Should he let her win, or force her hand?

He turned and started walking back up the hill. "Do as ye please, Lady Sophie."

"Wait. I didn't say you could leave."

"I dinna ask." As he continued his march up the hillside, he could hear her stirring behind him.

"But that's my horse. I summoned him," she yelled after him.

"I can walk. I ken the way." He could tell she had started to follow him; he heard her footsteps stomping the ground. He kept walking without turning around.

"Oooohhhh you . . . you . . . you human. It's a wonder I don't leave you here to wander on your own."

"Aye, 'tis a wonder, Lady Sophie."

She sprinted by him, holding handfuls of her skirt as she ran, and reached the horse afore him. "The horse will do my bidding. He will take you nowhere unless I say."

When he caught up to her, Herrick reached out to cup her face in his hands. "Ye are a wonder, Lady Sophie." Then he leaned forward and kissed her. He took her lips captive, willing her to feel the passion she provoked in him, the desire, the wanting, the longing to feel her body lying naked next to his. In return, he received a jolt of heated energy surging back at him. The sound of thunder rumbled through the clouds above. He looked up, expecting the sky to grow dark and stormy; but the sky remained blue, the clouds still fluffy and white.

She wrapped her arms around him, pulling him close. "You're asking for trouble."

"I'm sure I am." He brought his lips back down upon hers. The sound of thunder grew louder, and he realized 'twas the storm within Sophie he heard.

"You have no idea," she spoke breathlessly against his lips.

"I can only imagine."

Sophie broke away laughing. "Oh, my dearest Herrick. If you could only imagine the ecstasy such an act can create, but now is not the time, and here is not the place. I have great plans for you, Herrick of the clan MacNicol. 'Tis your turn to practice patience."

Enthralled by her sheer exuberance, yet bemused by her teasing nature, he lifted her up on the horse and took his place behind her. How right this had come to feel, traveling down the road with Sophie cradled in his arms. Listening to her laughter and fending off her temperamental bouts of emotions, both high and low, warmed his soul. And yet, she was still a mystery to him.

CHAPTER 5

They hadn't been back on the road for more than an hour when the weather took an unexpected turn for the worse. The blue sky and fluffy white clouds they had enjoyed only moments afore in the meadow were quickly being replaced with thick, dark rain clouds. A fierce wind was blowing in from the north, bringing with it thunder and lightning.

Sophie's safety was Herrick's first concern. He needed to find shelter for the night as soon as possible or risk being caught on the bare countryside without protection. The area they were traveling through was wide open, with nary a tree or bush in sight. Herrick directed Raynor off the pathway and headed at a gallop for the foothills. This took them out of their way, but not too far in the distance was a rocky cliff next to a fast running stream. Hopefully, he would find something there to shield them from the storm.

The rain had already started to fall by the time he found a narrow cave where they could camp for the night. It wasn't much more than a recessed niche with an extended ledge, but at least it provided shelter from the storm. Herrick positioned Raynor at the opening of the cave, using the beast's large body to serve as another wall of protection.

"I ken this isn't much, but it will have to do for now. At least it will keep us out of the rain. We'll have to do without a fire unless ye can summon flames from a rock."

"Nay. Such magic is beyond me," Sophie said through chattering teeth. Even with her cloak wrapped around her, the poor lass was shivering.

"Here, take my cloak," Herrick said as he draped it around her body. "Ye poor thing; ye are chilled to the bone."

"I wish I could simply summon another for you; but I am too cold and tired, and we are too far from any fields of sheep."

It shocked him to see how weakened she had become, and so quickly. It seemed a drop in temperature was all it took to drain her strength. This was another reminder she wasn't of his world. "Doona worry. I'm used to the cold, and I have my plaid to keep me warm."

"Perhaps we can share," she offered in a wee voice.

Herrick nodded. "Aye, we can share." There was a small space not marred with jutting rocks, and Herrick guided Sophie to sit there. "We won't be able to fully stretch out, but at least the ground beneath us is dry."

Sophie leaned against the wall of the cave and seemed to relax a bit. "I'll have you to keep me warm. As long as you are here, I will feel safe. Surely this storm cannot last. Surely it will be better tomorrow."

"Aye," Herrick agreed. "'Twill surely be better tomorrow."

He sat down next to Sophie and wrapped her in his arms. She looked worn out. They had been on the road for two days and with meager meals thanks to his aversion to letting her use her magick. Herrick was fairly certain she'd never had to endure such hardships in her world. He doubted she had ever gone hungry or slept anywhere other than her own comfortable bed. It also worried him to think this might be too much for her and as soon as she could gather her strength she would slip back through the veil separating their worlds, ending their time together. He hoped she wouldn't, but he knew he couldn't stop her.

As he brushed back a lock of damp hair from her face, he tried desperately to think of something to cheer her spirits. "Tomorrow, when this rain stops, I think we should do our best to summon a grand feast for ourselves. I'll gather wood for a fire, and ye can help me catch the biggest fish in that stream down below. It's been my experience a meal, any meal, always tastes best when one is hungry."

"That sounds grand, Herrick." Sophie managed a weak smile. "You make it sound grand. I shall look forward to this feast you speak of. And I shall enjoy another night of sleeping in your arms. Surely, at this moment, I could not ask for more."

He felt a shiver run through her and heard a low rumbling from her tummy. "Kenning yer imagination, I believe there is much more ye could think to desire."

"None of that is important. Right now all I desire is to sleep peacefully in your arms. That's not too much to ask, is it?" She looked up at him with her big doe eyes, and Herrick knew there was nothing he would deny her.

He admired her resolve. Many other women would have been sorely discomforted by the miserable cold, and would have made their complaints well known, but Sophie seemed resigned to accepting what nature had to throw at them.

~~~

Miserable, cold and hungry, Sophie wished she were lying in a warm, soft bed next to a roaring fire with a table laden with food nearby, but she would have none of that here. And though she also desperately wanted to leave Skye and return to the warmth of Avalee, she knew she couldn't. It wasn't because she couldn't use her magic to slip back through the veil and return home; it was because she refused to give up or give in to her weakness. She might not be big and strong like Herrick, or accustomed to living in his world—*damn* how the cold did drain her strength—but by the stars above, she was determined not to quit. This would not be where her story ended, for she would not run home at the first sight of pain and discomfort. Her adventure was not yet over.

She was also certain, as soon as she was able, she would summon the biggest and best feast either of them could imagine. Herrick had promised her as much, and she was going to make sure he kept his word.

Sophie stirred enough to take his cloak and drape it over the two of them before she snuggled back into his arms.

Amazingly, she could actually feel his body radiating heat, warming her up. Soon she felt drowsy, ready to drop off to sleep.

"Herrick, will you kiss me good night? I'd like to have something to take with me into my dreams."

"Aye, Lady Sophie, it would be my pleasure."

He kissed her sweetly, and gently, and she savored the moment. She sensed his desire and knew he wanted more, but imagined he controlled his passions in respect for her. It warmed her heart. Thoughts of making love to him flowed through her mind, but went no further. The spirit was willing, but the flesh was too weak. Besides, she reminded herself, now was not the time, and this certainly wasn't the proper place.

The next morning, much as Herrick had promised, they broke their long, imposed fast with a glorious feast of fresh fish, bread, ale, and cheese. Herrick encouraged Sophie to conjure up whatever she wanted, and with her help, he built a roaring fire; she had summoned the flame. It felt good to be warm, rested, and well fed. This was so much better than the night before. Herrick had come to accept that Lady Sophie's powers served her well and it was only fair she be allowed to put them to good use, especially after the ordeal she had already endured.

Hoping to lift her spirits, Herrick told her he expected a short day of travel, if all went well. So far on this journey, Herrick noted to himself, such was not always the case.

They were traveling along a ridge that ran high along the eastern shoreline and were on the final leg of their journey toward Portree when they came to a section of the road that had been washed away by a landslide. The recent heavy rains had caused a huge slice of ground to give way and plummet down the steep hillside, leaving a slippery slope of mud. What was left of the rain slicked path gave them little or nothing to grip, and less than ten paces to their left the land dropped sharply down a cliff to the ocean below. The greater concern to Herrick was the ledge of boulders sitting precariously above them. The heavy rains would have weakened the ground beneath them, but he figured they had held in place for this long, he could only hope they wouldn't choose now to come tumbling down.

Herrick surveyed the surrounding landscape and considered their options. He had hoped they would soon be home, but going around this washout would add another day to their journey. Having already put Sophie through so much, he couldn't ask her to agree to that. Maybe it was best for them to take their chances with what was left of this washed out road.

"It doesn't look good, but I think we can make it," Herrick said, trying to sound more confident than he felt.

"Are you sure it's safe to continue?" Sophie asked, looking as fearful as he felt.

"To be honest, I'm not sure." He had learned by now, 'twas best not to deceive her. "I think we should try. Our only other option is to go around; that will add another day to our journey." The look on Sophie's face told him that wasn't what she wanted to hear. "Mayhap you could ask Raynor if he can make it across this muddy ground with us on his back." He had come to accept Sophie's ability to converse with the animals.

Sophie paused a moment afore answering. "Honestly, we're not sure. Perhaps it would be better if we got down and walked."

Herrick looked down and examined her footwear. Little more than ankle boots, they didn't look sturdy enough to grip the slippery slope of the hillside. "I'm worried yer boots will slip in this mud."

She looked down at her feet and shrugged. "I care not if they are dirtied. I can always get others."

"'Tis their grip I am worried about. They doona look very sturdy."

"Oh," she nodded thoughtfully. "Will this be better?" He watched as her boots transformed into thicker, stronger leather.

"That should help." His own boots had seen better days, but he would make it work. They only needed to cover fifty or sixty feet of space afore they would be back on a solid path.

Sophie and Herrick slid off Raynor.

"I'd feel better if Raynor waited here 'til we are safely across," Herrick said. "He'll be more agile and able to cross on his own without us to slow him down."

"I think you're right," Sophie said.

Raynor's head bobbed in agreement.

Herrick shook his head in wonder. If someone had told him he would someday be speaking to a horse with the aid of a faerie, he would have deemed them fish-bait crazy, and yet, here he was. Time to keep moving forward. Herrick took Sophie's hand and inched his way onto the patch of muddy hillside. 'Twas every bit as slippery as he had feared, even more so.

Cautiously, they stepped out on what was left of the narrow ledge fronting the hillside. They were nearly on the other side, only a few more steps to go, when Herrick felt his feet slide out from under him.

Dang.

In one swift motion, he let go of Sophie's hand and turned his body to face the hillside, bending over to splay his hands on the ground to stop his fall. His actions set her off balance, and he heard her scream as she slid onto her backside in the mud.

From behind them, Raynor whinnied. At the same time, Herrick heard the crunching sound of rock moving against rock. The boulders perched overhead were giving way.

Herrick reached for Sophie and rolled hard toward the safety of the far side of the washout, trusting his momentum would be enough to carry them out of the path of the careening boulders without sending them over the cliff's edge. One of the large stones tumbled and crashed to the ground only inches from Sophie's back. Herrick yanked her across his body, away from the falling boulders, then shoved her towards drier ground. Still sliding towards the hillside's edge, he rolled onto his belly while scrambling to gain traction on the slick, slippery slope. His feet pumped the ground, seeking leverage with little success. He felt himself slowly slipping towards the steep cliff and the rock strewn beach below. Digging deeper into the muddy gravel, he finally managed to secure a foothold. He gave Sophie a final push ahead of him to safety then quickly crawled out after her.

"Holy Mother of God! That was close," Herrick cursed as he tried to catch his breath. "Are ye all right?" Sophie was splayed on the ground next to him, breathing heavy.

~~~

Gasping for breath, Sophie lay on the road next to Herrick. "I was scared, Herrick. More scared than I've ever been before."

He reached out his hand to touch her. "Umm, if ye doona mind, I think I'll just lie here for a few moments to catch my breath."

"Please," Sophie mumbled between gasps, "be my guest."

They continued to lie there a moment or two longer until Herrick recovered enough strength to scramble to his feet. "Are ye able to stand?" he asked.

Sophie managed to nod. "I think so."

He helped her to her feet. "Are ye all right?" he asked again, pulling her close.

She wrapped her arms around him and hung on. "You saved me, Herrick. You saved my life. I think I could have died." She trembled in his arms.

He reached down to cup her chin in his muddy palm. "I thought the fae were long-lived."

"Not against careening boulders and sheer cliffs." Breathing deep, she tried to control her shaky nerves.

Sophie wondered if the huge boulders or the far drop down the side of the cliff truly would have killed her. She had felt things here in this world she had never felt before: cold, hunger, and passionate desire. Now she could add bone crushing pain to the list. For certain, it seemed as though the boulder would have caused her deadly injury if Herrick had not yanked her out of its way. How easily she might have been crushed by its weight. As a visitor to this world, was she not also subject to its laws of nature? Not wanting to put her fae powers to such a test, Sophie reminded herself she needed to be careful while in the earthly realm.

Looking across the other side to check on Raynor, she saw him prancing in place and sensed he was nervous. "Can you make it, my mighty warrior?" she called out to him.

Raynor bobbed his head with seeming confidence.

"Please, be careful," she warned. Sophie couldn't help but be worried.

The steed nodded again and sent her a wave of strong animal assurance.

Herrick and Sophie backed down the road to give him room to cross.

Strong and agile, Raynor safely trekked his way across the muddy hillside. When he reached their side, Sophie reached out and hugged his neck. "You are the best horse ever."

Raynor whinnied his approval and swished his long, glorious tail.

Pulling back from the grey gelding, Sophie saw she had left behind a blot of mud. She looked over at Herrick then down at herself and started to laugh. "We're a sodden, muddy mess. Think you can find us a stream in which we can wash?" She took her hands and ran them down the side of his face, leaving muddy streaks.

"Aye, my lady. Think ye can summon soap and a warm gust of wind to dry us when we do?" Herrick scooped a glob of mud from his chest and ran his dirty finger down the bridge of her nose.

"I'll see what I can do," she said, wiping tears of joy from her face with the back of her hand. Surely there wasn't an inch of her that wasn't covered in mud.

"My beautiful Lady Sophie." Herrick pulled her close and kissed her hard.

Sophie sent a prayer of thanks to the stars above. They were alive, and it was blessedly good to be alive. She had experienced a terrible fright, but the only thing that mattered was that they had survived, and thankfully without serious harm. Injuries were one problem she believed she still had the power to heal, but death, not so much.

Herrick had been fiercely determined to save them both, and she had to admit, there was something to be said for fierce determination.

They mounted Raynor and headed down the road. A moment later, Herrick directed the horse to take off across an open field towards a hidden valley where he knew he would find a natural pool concealed in a glen of heather and popular trees. The place was a ways off the well-traveled path, and he was counting on a wee bit of privacy. The idea that Lady Sophie would strip down to bathe spurred him to instruct Raynor to go faster.

"Only in consideration of yer comfort, my Lady," he said as the horse broke into a gallop.

"As if I don't know," Lady Sophie said laughingly, causing Herrick to wonder if she had read his thoughts. "I'm sure you're as uncomfortable as I am covered in this mud."

She had guessed wrong, but Herrick could only laugh. "Aye, my lady."

When they reached the glen, Herrick helped Sophie down from the horse and held her close in front of him, capturing her gaze in his.

"Do ye need help undressing?" His voice rumbled low in his chest.

Sophie brought her hands up to the laces of his linen tunic. "No more than you, I imagine."

Herrick wiped his hands down the front of his shirt afore reaching for the ribbon lacing up the front of her dress. "Fair is fair."

Slowly, with laughing eyes, they pealed the sodden layers of clothing from each other. Sophie undid the buckle on his belt, dropping it and his heavy sword to the ground. She pulled his wet tunic up over his head and tossed it into the pool.

"Impressive," she sighed.

Herrick loosened the stays of her gown and slid it down off her shoulders to reveal her breasts.

"Perfection," he murmured, and kissed her again.

With his help, she unfurled the length of plaid that covered his body then stepped out of the skirts of her dress, adding them to the pile floating at the water's edge for later washing. Soon they both stood naked at the side of the pool.

Sophie shivered. "How cold do you think it is?" she asked, still holding his gaze.

"How warm do ye want it to be? This is one time I would be grateful for yer fae magick to heat things up . . . in the water, I mean." He was already standing at attention and rock hard, needing no more magick from his wee faerie than the mere sight of her provided.

She stretched out a long graceful leg and dipped her toe into the pool, holding it there until she seemed satisfied with the results. "Does this please you?"

Herrick stepped to the water's edge. It was hotter than the warmest bathwater he had ever enjoyed. It would be heaven. "Everything about ye pleases me."

He led her into the pool and sank down to sit on the rocky bottom. The heated water massaging his aching limbs made him moan with undisguised pleasure. "I have reached Valhalla."

"Not yet, my warrior prince, but you soon will," Sophie purred. She ran her hands over his chest and shoulders, bringing added heat to his skin.

He pulled her to sit atop of him, straddling his thighs, his hand grasping her softly rounded bottom. Then he ran his fingers through the braid of her sliver-blond hair until 'twas loose and floating freely upon the surface of the water like finely spun lace. Sophie arched her back to dip her head in the water and her breasts pointed skyward. Herrick lowered his mouth to suckle the tight pink buds of her hardened nipples. She moaned with pleasure. He brought her close and kissed his way up her neck, chin, cheeks, and her lush, full, pink lips then he kissed every inch of her beautiful white skin while his rough and calloused hands roamed freely over her soft silken body.

When he could wait no longer, when he felt her need and desire for him exceed his own, he brought her up close and positioned her over his hardened shaft. She wrapped her legs around his waist, assisting his effort, and together they became one, joined in a sensual connection of bliss. His thrusting was hard and urgent, as if he were searching for something floating just beyond his grasp. Relentlessly, he pushed on, seeking her joy, her pleasure, her release. As he thrust inside her, he felt her ecstasy open wide, and his senses burst forth with an array of colored lights. Music filled the air.

Never afore had lovemaking felt this good.

This, his soul screamed, was something new, never experienced afore. This was more than a base desire to please himself and this beautiful woman. This was more than a simple exchange of pleasure. Something deeper was taking place, of that he was sure, but he had no words. These feelings and sensations were all too new to him.

With a final thrust, his soul shattered, and he felt as if he'd been hurled from his body to the far reaches of space. The stars and the moon went whizzing by as he ascended higher and higher until finally he reached the pinnacle of pleasure and then floated back down in liquid ecstasy.

He lay limp against the moss covered rocks. It took a moment afore he was able to speak. "What in heaven did ye do to me?"

Sophie's smile was wicked. "I told you . . . I warned you. When I make love, I don't hold back."

"Right. I seem to recall something about that."

Together they floated in the steaming water and crept to the water's edge. He was all done in.

Sophie held up her hand and showed him a cake of soap and a washing cloth. "Isn't this what we came here for?"

Herrick nodded. "Right ye are. Have at it." Restfully lounging at the water's edge, he enjoyed every minute of Sophie's care as she washed his hair, face, and every inch of his body. A more pleasurable bath had surely never been had by man or fae.

"You're a fine, brawn man," Sophie said, as she rubbed the soap across his broad shoulders and down his back.

"And ye are a fine, supple woman," Herrick replied, enjoying every touch of her hands.

"Together, I think we make a mighty, fine couple," she said, reaching around to rub soap on his chest as her breasts pressed against his back.

Herrick held his breath, wondering what she might mean.

"It's a shame you're not of my world," she sighed, resting her head upon his back.

Herrick released his breath and tucked away his desire. *And ye are not of mine,* he reminded himself.

With quiet efficiency, they finished washing and were soon dressed again, their clothes clean and dried by Sophie's magick. It was time to get back on the road headed towards home—his home—where Sophie would undoubtedly leave him. Herrick didn't want to think about that now; not after the bliss she had shown him. He needed something else to occupy his mind.

"Ye have told me very little about yer life on Avalee. I have answered yer questions. Now 'tis time for ye to answer mine. Agreed?" Maybe hearing her speak would take his mind off his worries.

Sophie gazed at him with teasing eyes and pouted—oh how those lips begged to be kissed.

"I shall try," she said. "But if you ask a question I cannot answer, well, then I cannot answer."

"Fair enough. What can ye tell me about yer childhood? What was it like growing up as a fae?"

She sighed dreamily and smiled as she moved closer, leaning cozily into his chest. "It was full of dancing and music and play. We lived in a big, grand house. Bigger and more beautiful than any you could imagine. I was always surrounded by people who loved and cared for me. As a child, very little was expected of me other than to learn my lessons and enjoy my life."

Herrick had been born and raised in a humble cottage. Nothing in his life could be described as beautiful or grand until he met her. His training to become a warrior had begun afore he turned eight.

"What lessons are the fae taught?" he asked.

"How to love and laugh and live. How to sing and dance. We are taught to enjoy each day and the blessings it brings. We also learn, I suppose from watching our elders, what it's like to have power: the kind of power that comes with position and beauty and wealth. Every faerie has all they need, some simply have more."

He, too, had learned about power: the power of the sword and the rightness of might. As a Scot, but even more so as a nephew to his clan's chief, he had also learned the importance of a strong clan.

"What about yer family? Tell me about them. Have ye any siblings?"

"My family is large. I have six sisters; I am the youngest. My parents each have several brothers and sisters, and I have more aunts and uncles and cousins than can be counted with the stars of heaven. We are all close—sometimes too close—and gather together often. We celebrate everything with grand feasts, and there is always wine to drink."

"And cheese and grapes?" he asked, remembering their first night together.

"Yes, and cheese and grapes, and meats and breads. A large man, such as you, could eat his fill, and still there would be plenty more."

"What could I possibly offer to compare? This is not even my horse." Herrick chuckled as he spoke, but 'twas only for show. Her description of her world weighed heavy upon his heart. She was part of a large and strong clan, one that could provide for her every need, wish, or desire. He could offer little more than a warm hut and a full belly, and oftentimes, much less than even that.

"If the meaning of precious is something rare, then I believe I have experienced something precious indeed," Sophie said. She looked at him with an upturned face, but he read sadness in her eyes. 'Twas obvious she missed the pleasures of home.

Herrick had never seen a feast such as she described. On earth, the effort to have even enough was always a struggle. Beautiful and bountiful as Mother Earth was, it could never compete with the land of the fae. Earth was rough and harsh, and as Sophie had often said, always cold. He felt her snuggle close to him, presumably for warmth, and was reminded she wasn't of his world. Herrick felt a tightening in his chest, as if someone had reached in to grab ahold of his heart.

A miserable drizzling rain started again shortly afore the sunset, darkening the sky with thick grey clouds and chilling them to their bones. Their time at the pool had caused a greater delay than Herrick had planned and they needed to stop for the night. This time, Herrick was able to find a shepherd's hut nestled along the rocky hillside. 'Twas little more than three walls of rock piled high enough to break the wind with a poorly thatched roof and a dirt floor, but he was grateful for the shelter it provided. With Sophie's help, Herrick caught a rabbit to go with the wild berries he had gathered along the way. She also conjured up some wine, bread, and cheese, saying 'twas all they needed.

Herrick watched her eat the simple fare and wished he could give her more. She came from a land of plenty. 'Twas very unlikely she found their meager meal satisfying or filling. Nonetheless, she didn't complain or ask for more.

As they took their places lying next to each other in the darkness of the night, a sense of unease settled over Herrick. Tomorrow they would reach Scorrybreac. In truth, alone he would have already covered the distance, but he had lingered on their journey, enjoying every moment he spent with Lady Sophie.

She nestled up close to his chest, and he cradled her in his arms as he felt her drift off to sleep. Neither of them attempted to arouse the other to passion. 'Twas as if they shared an unspoken understanding that what they had experienced earlier couldn't be repeated, at least not here, not now, surrounded by the dark, wet, and cold.

Maybe she was simply tired from living life as a human, from being too cold and too hungry. At times, he had seen her energy fade, as if simply being here in his world were too much for her, but he suspected 'twas something more. It seemed as if she were ready for her adventure to end.

Dearest Sophie, he thought, darling Lady Sophie. She was a boon he didn't deserve. Much like the mists that were a near constant companion to the Isle of Skye, she couldn't be contained. She would come and go as she pleased. Here today; but what about tomorrow? Or the next day? When would she decide her adventure was over and 'twas time for her to go home? It could not be long now. Soon her story would have a proper ending. He expected when they arrived at the home of his family, she would see her adventure was over and would say good-bye. The dreary workaday life of a Scotsmen on the cold and damp Isle of Skye was no place for a faerie princess such as her.

~~~

Sophie snuggled next to Herrick, more for his comfort than for his warmth; although, his body was like a furnace that gave great heat. It didn't take magic to read his thoughts, for she was sure hers were nearly the same. Regardless of the bond they shared, her adventure would soon come to an end.

Tomorrow they would be back among his people, where he lived, and she could not stay. She was fae, and the fae did not live in the world of the humans. Already, she was pushing her luck, hoping her sisters would not notice her absence or feel the effects of her making love with Herrick. Surely their union had resonated through the heavens. She only hoped the pool of water had helped to absorb their soul-shattering vibrations, but it could not be long now. Another day, two at best, and she would need to return to Avalee.

Earlier, at the pool, Sophie had tried to hold back, really she had, but Herrick had taken control, pushing her higher, demanding from her all she had to give. She had hoped to wait, planning to make their joining her farewell gift to him. But once a gift was given it could not be taken back.

She wondered if anyone back home on Avalee had felt effects of their union.

Interestingly, she had no great desire to tell her tale to her sisters, or the queen, or anyone else. Her time with Herrick would not be used to entertain the fae court. Even though this was truly the first grand adventure of her life, she had no desire to flaunt her time with Herrick for the pleasure of others. She understood now, better than she ever had before, the pleasure of a secret; something only she knew and held in her heart. It was a secret she had not even shared with Herrick. A tear trickled from her eye, and she felt it fall along her cheek. She had committed the most unacceptable act a faerie ever could, yet she had no regrets. No one else needed to know she was falling in love with a human.

CHAPTER 6

Herrick was both excited and apprehensive. Soon they would be home, at his mother's cottage near Scorrybreac. Would this be the end of their journey together? Would Sophie leave him now and return to her friends to tell her tale of how she saved a Scottish Highland warrior from near death and returned him safely to his family's home? Did she know, that when she left, he would be doomed to live out the rest of his miserable days with only the memory of her beauty and laughter and fierce little temper to brighten his dreary life? For life surely would be dreary without her.

But she was fae, and he was human; 'twas best he keep that in mind. They lived in separate worlds. Their paths had crossed by mere chance because of Sophie's whimsical notion to go on an adventure so she could have a story to tell her friends back home on Avalee.

When they reached a point in the road where they could see his home, he brought the horse to a halt.

"There, Lady Sophie, that cottage over yonder is my home. And down below near the shore is the village of Portree."

She looked out over the countryside. "The view must be grand, but why do you choose to live such a distance from the village? Isn't it safer to be near other humans?"

"My mother is often uncomfortable around others. She prefers her privacy." Actually, it was the others who were uncomfortable around her. Too often she had foretold of events to come, and this caused many of the village folk to shun her. The future, they said, was best left to the will of God and not spied upon by mere mortals. Over time, she learned to quell her desire to help others with her gift of sight; choosing instead to live apart to avoid their stares and whispered gossip.

Herrick's mouth suddenly became dry, and he found it difficult to speak. He cleared his throat. "Ye have brought me safely home, Lady Sophie. Is this not a fitting ending to yer tale of adventure?"

"Certainly, you would not expect me to leave before I meet your mother. Or are you too proud to admit it was a woman who saved your nearly dead ass and saw you safely home? Are you too ashamed of me to let us meet?"

"Ye speak nonsense," he barked. Ire spiked through Herrick. He was not ungrateful, he was simply trying to let her go gracefully.

Sophie pulled back, glaring. "Do I?"

"Ye have said from the beginning, ye plan to leave me."

"I'll leave you when I'm damn well good and ready, and not a minute before. So, are we going to stand here and argue, or are you going to let me meet your mother?"

Dang, for a sweet little faerie, she sure was bossy. He rather liked that about her. A grin spread across Herrick's face as he brought his anger back under control. "Twould be my pleasure and my honor to introduce ye to Ma. I think 'tis only fair to say, although I think ye ken by now, my mother has the gift of sight. I would be surprised if she does not see ye for who ye truly are."

Sophie smiled and shrugged, her usual response. "I expected as much. I'm sure you can understand my curiosity. I have never before met a human with such a gift."

Herrick eyed her with skepticism. "Mary Duffie has such a gift."

She gave another shrug. "Yes, but I respected her desire to keep it hidden. I am hoping your mother will be, shall we say, more willing to share. After all, I am returning her son to her, hale and hearty."

"Ma will welcome yer presence with open arms. Come, let us finish our journey. I expect Raynor will leave us now and return to his master."

"Actually, no, he is yours to keep. It turns out his master has been absent for several days. Raynor and I agree, it's very likely he was lost in the Viking raid that caused you such injury."

"A horse told ye all that?" he asked with disbelief.

Sophie laughed merrily. "Yes and no. I have other ways of gathering information. Remember how a little birdie told me of Mary Duffie's cottage? I was speaking true when I told you that."

"A most convenient talent, to be sure."

He spurred the horse forward to finish the final steps of their journey. At the front door of his cottage, he helped Sophie down and gave her time to set herself to rights afore they went in. She adorned herself once more in the gossamer blue gown she had worn when he first met her on the beach. Her long blond hair was pulled back from her face, and the royal blue cloak hung over her shoulders. There could be no mistaken she was anything other than fae.

As they were about to enter the cottage, Sophie pointed off through the crop of surrounding trees and asked, "Who lives in that cottage over there? It looks unkempt compared to this one."

Herrick looked to where she was pointing and quickly turned away. "'Tis only in need of repair."

"Hmm! What would it take to make it whole again?" Sophie asked.

Herrick glanced over his shoulder. "A family."

Mable MacNicol sat quietly in her chair, waiting for her son to arrive. A meal had been prepared of roasted pig and turnips to be served with freshly baked bread spread with creamy butter and slabs of cheese. Ale sat in a cooled pitcher, ready to be poured into mugs. Any minute now he would walk through the door. Of that, she was sure.

She thanked the stars above and his sainted father that Herrick had been allowed to survive the Viking raid and return home. Mable had kenned he was walking into trouble when he went down to the village with his uncle, but she had also knew it not her place to stop him. The fates had something grander planned for her son, and she needed to trust he would survive the test.

What Mable wondered about most was the person coming home with him. Who was it that had accompanied her son on his journey? She saw the presence of another in his life, and she was fairly certain *who* she was, but until she could see the woman with her own eyes, she wouldn't be convinced this particular vision were true.

A moment later, the door opened, and her son appeared, hale and hearty. He ducked as he stepped into the room, filling the cottage with his presence. It did her heart good to see him again. She rose from her chair and took him in her arms, embracing her adult son as if he were still the lad of his youth. Oh, how it did her heart good to hold him.

"Ma, I'm home. I've returned from the raid, and I've brought someone with me. Someone I want ye to meet." He stepped aside, and into her humble cottage walked the most beautiful faerie she had ever seen. She stood, regal and proud, revealing the full strength of her glamor.

Mable bowed in deep respect to the princess who stood afore her. "My Lady," she said.

"Mistress Mable, it is an honor to finally meet you. It has been my great joy to accompany your son as he returned home to you."

Herrick, God bless his soul, stood with his mouth agape, looking dumfounded.

"Ye must ken she is fae," Mable said to her son. It amused her to see him looking so dazed. No doubt her strong, handsome son had been brought low by the stunning beauty of this faerie princess.

The faerie princess smiled brightly and said, "She has been expecting us. Am I not right, Mistress Mable?"

"Ye are correct. Come, ye must be tired and hungry. I have prepared a meal. 'Tis not much, but I hope 'twill be welcomed."

"Your efforts are greatly appreciated," the princess said.

"As are yers, Lady . . ."

"Sophie," Herrick offered, apparently recovering his wits. "Lady Sophie of the fae, this is my mother, Mistress Mable of the MacNicols."

"You did that well," Lady Sophie said quietly to Herrick.

His smiling face reminded Mable of a young lad in training being given his first real sword. She grinned proudly. "I am honored," she said with another slight bow.

"As am I," Lady Sophie replied.

Mable wondered if her son knew he was in the presence of a faerie princess. It appeared he didn't. It also appeared the two had become very friendly while on their journey together. She saw the light of the fae shining bright in his emerald-green eyes and knew they had shared more than friendship during their time together. She knew the mark of the fae when she saw it. She also knew her efforts to get Herrick's cottage cleaned and ready for guests had been worth the pain, and thanked the stars above she had been so inspired.

"Come, let us eat and drink. I have prepared a table for ye. 'Tis simple fare, but ye shall not go hungry." Mable gestured to the dining table. As they took their seats, she poured the ale. "Tell me, my son, how did ye survive?"

Herrick sat at the head of the table and began to carve the hank of roasted pig. "The fighting was brutal; I'm sure I need not tell ye about that. Many were gravely injured, others dead. I took a beating myself. One blow I thought to be fatal, but I survived. I was able to return to the beachhead and take the one remaining boat to bring me back to Skye. 'Twas barely seaworthy, but I was blessed with calm waters and a favorable tide. My only wish was to return home to Skye afore I should die. I had no desire to perish on the Isle of Harris among the enemy."

"As I recall, that wasn't your only wish," Lady Sophie said, smiling.

"Surely ye were blessed from above," Mable commented, wondering how close her son and this faerie princess had become.

Turning bright, smiling eyes to their guest, he continued. "Lady Sophie found me on the beach and healed my wounds. She summoned a mighty steed to ease our travel and gave me great joy along the way. Had it not been for her, I might still be lying on the beach where she found me, bereft of life."

"Saints above, I have not enough words to thank ye," Mable said to Lady Sophie.

"I can assure you, Mistress Mable, it has been my pleasure." Like true royalty, Lady Sophie humbly accepted her gratitude.

Mable took a moment to gather her thoughts. 'Twas time to deliver the news to her son, and let him know his life was more changed than he might imagine. "Herrick, yer Uncle Nicail dinna make it back. He was lost in the raid that nearly took yer life. The clan has been waiting, hoping ye would return. They expect ye to be the next MacNicol chief."

Herrick abruptly rose from his chair. It fell back with a clatter. "Chief of our clan? Me?"

Mable bid him to sit back down. "Ye have survived where others have fallen. This is yer destiny, Herrick."

Her son set the chair to rights then sat with his forearms upon the table and leaned forward. The look on his face was a mixture of fear and amazement. "How could they even ken I survived? I've only just arrived home?"

Mable met his gaze steadily. "I told them. They came to me and asked."

~~~

Herrick sat back in his chair, amazed, dumbfounded, and bewildered. To think his kinsmen had come to his mother, seeking her visions and advice, spoke greatly of their need for leadership and direction. His uncle had two sons, but it seemed both had been lost in the battle. He feared they hadn't survived, though he had held out hope for his uncle. Not only was that hope crushed, but in its place was the realization of the burden now placed upon him.

He stared off into space, not really tasting the food he placed in his mouth; although, he was fairly certain the roasted pig was blessedly delicious. Besides being a seer, his mother was an amazing cook.

What on earth was he supposed to do as chief of his clan? What did his kinsmen expect of him? Did his responsibilities begin now, or in the morning when he awoke, or had they already begun? He had so many questions, and yet so few answers.

Herrick looked across the table at his mother, and a feeling of calm came over him. If anyone could counsel him through these rough seas, 'twas Mable MacNicol. That woman would see him through the darkest storms. Suddenly he knew he had naught to worry, at least not until he had to actually show up to be a leader for his clan.

When their meal was done, Herrick rose from his chair to help his mother.

"Leave it be," she said to him. "I will tend to the chores. In anticipation of yer return, I have prepared yer cottage. Ye will sleep there tonight. There is a pile of peat for yer fire and quilts a plenty on the bed to keep ye warm." His mother then turned to Lady Sophie and said, "Ye are welcome to anything I have to offer."

Sophie smiled serenely. "Your hospitality is most graciously accepted. You shall have the blessing of my gratitude all the days of your life."

"I am humbled by yer blessing. Thank ye for bringing my son home. That alone was blessing enough." Mable stood and began clearing the table. "'Tis getting dark; ye best take a lamp to light yer way."

She was telling him it was time to go. And she understood Sophie would go with him.

Although slightly bigger, his cottage was much like his mother's with the living space in the front and the sleeping area near the back. There was a large fireplace between the two areas to warm the cottage and cook their food.

"Welcome to my humble abode," Herrick said as he led Sophie through the front door. "'Tis better than anything we've had along the road, but I expect it falls woefully short of anything ye have in Avalee."

Sophie took a look around the room, appraising her surroundings. "Herrick, my dear, I can assure you, your mere presence makes this humble cottage a castle." The look in her eyes radiated love and appreciation.

"Ye are too kind, but I confess, it fills me with pride to hear ye approve of my humble abode. Ye are more than I deserve."

"That's not possible." She smiled, and the room seemed to grow brighter.

Herrick wondered if he should offer her a drink or something to eat, although he couldn't imagine either one of them needed anything after the meal his mother had served. Then again, maybe he could use a drink. He went to the plain wooden cupboard where he stored his best whisky. Actually, 'twas his only bottle of whisky. "I think I shall have a wee bit of the dram, would ye like to join me? Should I pour ye a drink?"

She nodded, "As you wish."

Sophie walked over to the sleeping area. The bed was nicely made up and covered with handmade woolen quilts, thanks to the thoughtfulness of his mother. "Is this where we shall sleep?"

Herrick nodded and took a deep swallow from his pewter mug.

"Would you mind if I made a few adjustments?" she asked, glancing over her shoulder.

"Make yerself at home," he said, well aware this could be nothing like her home.

With a wave of her hand, the simple rope-tied bed and ticking mattress turned into a large four-poster bed with a thick wool-stuffed mattress covered in feather and down quilts. With another wave of her hand, Sophie's clothes dropped away, and she lay unclothed atop the jewel colored silken sheets.

Herrick nearly choked on his drink. "Quite an improvement."

"I'm glad you approve. It is as I have imagined, and I believe you understand how strong my imagination can be."

"Whatever ye can imagine, ye can create, am I not right?"

Her smile became playful. "Something like that."

~*~

A few minutes later, though not nearly as quickly as Sophie would have liked, Herrick stood proud and naked before her. The fire light danced off her alabaster skin while Herrick's bronze, sun-kissed skin reflected the heat of the flames. Herrick slipped onto the bed beside her as she welcomed him with open arms. Wrapping her arms around him, she leaned in to kiss his lips. He tasted of earthy spices and a hint of the whisky he recently drank. The magnificence of his human body was beyond anything she could have imagined. Adam's tales never included anything like this. He kissed her, and a surge of passion shot through them both, heating their skin and filling her with power. Tonight, she was in control, and their passion was about to become everything he could imagine, and more.

The air around them took on a pulsating glow, dancing with every color of the rainbow. The fragrance of flowers filled the air as it grew warm and sultry. She felt the vortex forming around them, and she did nothing to stop it. Wrapping her arms around his neck, she ran her fingers through his thick, ginger hair and held him close as she welcomed his kiss with matching desire.

"Tonight, my warrior prince, you shall see Valhalla," Sophie purred. She ran her hands over his chest and shoulders and felt the heat burning through his skin. Absorbed in her desire, she let her fingers slide down to the taut muscles of his abdomen, mesmerized by the feel of his skin as heat radiated from his body. She sensed he was exerting incredible control for her benefit, and she loved him all the more for his care.

He kissed her again, softly at first, teasing her senses into heightened awareness. His hands moved slowly and methodically along the length of her, as if exploring new uncharted territory for the first time while learning every curve of her shapely body. He moved his hands along her long slender legs and up across her abdomen. He reached to grasp the fullness of her breasts, kissing and suckling the rosy nipples until her body strained for release from the sensual torture.

"Herrick," she called out his name, "Please, Herrick."

"Good Lord! Woman, ye truly are beautiful."

She snaked her arms around his back and bound him to her with a steely grip. "Let me feel your strength," she declared, seeking their carnal connection.

"My sweet, darling Lady Sophie," Herrick moaned. "Ye are everything I could ever want in my life." He held her close, fueling her lust, even as she felt him bursting with a need of his own.

He continued his exploration, touching her, stroking her, savoring her wet readiness as he rubbed, teased, and tormented her with sensual arousal.

Herrick's eyes took on a predatory gleam. It was obvious he could wait no longer. Sophie's body cried out for him as he moved to position himself between her thighs, pausing one sweet moment longer in anticipation before he sank himself deep inside her. Her muscles clenched around him in response to their joining. Sacred pleasure tumbled through her in shuttering waves as she moaned in lustful delight.

Sophie pulled her legs up to wrap around his waist, fully welcoming and embracing his body with her own.

Never before had she experienced this soulful connection with another as their two bodies united to become one in an intimate lovers embrace. Colorful lights swirled around them, dancing and twinkling in tune with her delight.

She felt him move within her, slowly at first, but then gaining momentum to create a rhythmic thrust and pull that stirred her senses. She matched his rhythm, moving in sync, building a mounting force of pleasure. Their soul-searing bliss continued to climb until their bodies peaked in sensual ecstasy with a brilliant explosion of passion.

Sophie felt the great strength of their vibrational disturbance as it thundered through her and knew it couldn't possibly go unnoticed in Avalee. Together they had roared through the heavens, touched the stars, and bathed in moon dust. It was a moment of pure joining, everything she had hoped it would be and more. She had soared to the stars and now felt light as a feather drifting lazily back down to earth with a more loving feeling than even she had imagined.

Satiated by their intense release of pleasure and pent-up passions, Herrick collapsed into her arms and rolled to his side. It was a long moment before either was able to speak as they worked to slow their labored breathing. Herrick pulled Sophie to face him as he kissed her again, and again.

"Words canna describe," he mumbled, shaking his head.

She searched his eyes and saw her mark locked deep within. A gift given could not be returned; he was hers forever. No other woman would ever be able to claim him as she just had. Her eyes filled with bittersweet tears of joy, knowing she would hold this moment in her heart forever.

Herrick felt as though his heart would burst through his chest. "I shall love ye forever," he whispered in adoring surrender as he gazed upon her with awe. He had let go of his will to resist, and in doing so, he had succumbed to Sophie's alchemy of intimacy. Nothing afore her had ever felt this good, this amazing. Nothing else ever would. She had changed him forever more.

Sophie smiled brilliantly, deeply comforted by the sureness in his voice and his words, both spoken and unspoken. She had no idea what tomorrow would bring, but for this one bright shining moment in time, she knew she was supremely happy. Nothing more needed to be said as she lay there in his arms.

She curled up next to him in complete exhaustion with his body draped over hers in nocturnal protection. Delighting in the feel of their naked bodies entwined in a lovers embrace, Sophie fell blissfully asleep.

CHAPTER 7

Falling. Sophie was sleeping, snuggled safe and warm next to Herrick, when she suddenly felt herself falling—falling from his arms, falling from his bed, falling away from him. Or was she being pulled? Yes, that was it. She was being pulled; she was being pulled back behind the veil.

When the sensation of movement ended, she found herself lying naked in a heap at the feet of her eldest sister, the queen. Sunlight filtered through the floor-to-ceiling windows encasing the room and reflected brightly off the white marble columns lining the terrace. A warm sultry breeze heated the air. Everything in the room pulsed with a faint golden glow. There was only one place she could be: the private chambers of her sister Queen Danu. Looking about, she saw her other five sisters were also present.

"Must my disgrace be made public?" Sophie asked Danu, her eldest sister.

"Your sisters and I hardly constitute a public shaming, but such can be arranged if you would like," Queen Danu said. Gracefully, she moved a few paces away to lounge on a silk covered divan that perfectly matched her silver-white gown. Sophie had to admit, as queen of the fae, her sister was quite an impressive sight.

"Oh, like none of you have ever visited the realm of the humans." Sophie sat up on the floor and took stock of her sisters. They weren't happy, none of them were smiling, but it could be worse. They could be laughing.

Sindi, the second oldest, took the seat next to Danu. She wore a sheer gown in a blazing shade of red that perfectly complemented her evil green eyes and envious complexion.

Vanella, Quella, and Renalee all sat together on the only sofa in the room. They each wore lovely, natural shades of peach, lemon, and lime that suited them to perfection. As the three middle sisters, they were kind and quiet and tended to stay bunched together. Sophie wondered if it were by choice or because the family simply saw them as one.

Like the rest of her sisters, the second youngest, Amora, also took a seat on one of the plush covered armchairs forming a circle around Sophie. She wore an unflattering gown in a sad shade of purple, which would have been better left in her closet, or perhaps tossed on the floor, or even better, used as a rag.

"We've all visited their realm, but not one of us has ever been so brazen, so bold, or so foolish as to fall in love with one of them," Sindi offered, shaking her head.

"Too bad for you. You should try it sometime," Sophie said as she stood and dressed herself in a shimmery blue gown. If she were going to be put to shame, she might as well look good for the party.

"What shall we do with her, sisters?" Danu asked calmly—a little too calmly, it seemed. Sophie wondered about that.

"Shall we send her to the kitchens, the gardens, or perhaps the workshops to serve her punishment?" Amora asked. Considering she was only a decade older than Sophie, Amora seemed to be enjoying this tribunal a bit too much.

"Excuse me! What punishment is this you speak of? Have I already been tried and found guilty?" Sophie enquired, becoming more and more concerned.

"Do you deny you made love to a human?" Sindi asked.

"Well, no." She was pretty sure it wouldn't do any good to try and deny her actions. There was no reason to believe the sensual vibrations she had created with Herrick hadn't also been felt here in Avalee by one or more of her sisters, especially Sindi. She lived for such occasions. "But, in my defense, I've never known that to be a problem for the fae."

"Making love to most anyone is not a problem for the fae," Danu said languidly.

"Making love to a human because you have fallen in love with him is quite a different thing. Wouldn't you agree, sisters?" Sindi asked, looking at her sisters for confirmation.

Amora nodded in agreement. The others merely shrugged.

As usual, Queen Danu seemed only mildly interested, but with her eldest sister, outward appearances were often deceiving.

Apparently Sindi was to serve as her interrogator. Sophie wondered if her role were self-designated or if this arrangement was under Danu's request.

"I have no regrets," Sophie said with a lift of her chin. She combed her fingers through her hair and fluffed it out, hoping to rid herself of any residual traces of bedhead.

"You have no scruples," Sindi spat out.

"Oh, please! Must you be so melodramatic?" Sophie rolled her eyes. Standing in the middle of the circle, surrounded by her sisters, she noticed there was no place for her to sit. So be it; that was fine with her. "I stand by my actions," she declared, resisting the urge to stomp her foot. It was time to demonstrate to her sisters she had done some maturing. "I went to the aid of a human. At the time, it seemed like the right thing to do. I admit I experienced feelings of compassion, desire, even love in ways I never have before, but I have no regrets. I believe I am better for having known him."

"Now you're the one being melodramatic," Amora laughed.

Sophie wanted to tell Amora to shut up and butt out. "Tell me how I am to amend for this *grievous* offense, and let's be done with this. I'd like to take a hot bath and go back to bed, to sleep, which is what I was doing before I was so rudely yanked back here."

119

Danu looked at her with what looked like a hint of compassion. "Dear Sophie, if only it could be so simple."

"You're not going to let her get away with this, are you Danu?" Sindi questioned, and then, after seeing the disapproving look she got from her older sister, she added, "My queen."

"It would be best if you didn't plan any more trips to the earthly realm for a decade or two," Queen Danu said to Sophie rather unceremoniously.

"What? Am I being grounded? Like a child?" *Oh pooh*, it looked as if she were going to get more than a simple slap upon her knuckles. "I'm nearly two hundred years old. I think I'm capable of . . . of . . . better than that."

Sindi grinned at her viciously. "The queen has spoken." Judging by the gleeful look in her eyes, she seemed to be enjoying this far too much. Apparently, she was still smarting over the time Sophie had teased her about getting stood up by Zepher, one of the most desired fae in all of Avalee.

Amora nodded in full agreement with Sindi while Vanella, Quella, and Renalee simply stared at her wide-eyed, probably grateful it wasn't them attracting the attention of their two older sisters.

Queen Danu took a look around the circle and said, "Sisters, I believe I need to speak with Sophie in private."

Her sisters exchanged questioning glances, but Danu gave a wave of her slender hand, and each of her sisters stood to leave, except Sindi. She remained seated.

"You too, Sindi." Danu eyed her next younger sister with royal resolve.

"But I'm the one who . . ."

"You have done enough. You can leave now," Danu reaffirmed ever so softly.

That confirmed it, Sophie had little doubt it was Sindi who had taken notice of her vibrational union with Herrick and reported it to Danu. Not that it mattered much, one way or the other. The damage was done.

When everyone was gone, Danu gestured for Sophie to take a seat.

"Dearest little sister, you're the baby of the family. I wonder if we haven't allowed you a bit too much freedom to do as you please. Or have we ignored you and by doing so underestimated your needs. I believe we may have been remiss in our attentions to you."

This was the first time Danu had taken the time to speak to her directly, alone, one on one, as if she cared. Sophie wondered how she should react. She decided to be honest. "I mean what I said, my queen. I'm sorry if I have displeased you, but I have no regrets."

Danu sighed prettily. "Earth—the world of humans—is not a pretty place, not an easy place, especially not for one such as you."

"With all respect, my queen, I believe you are wrong. Granted, it is not like Avalee. Nothing can compare to the beauty of our home, but the world of earth has its own sort of beauty. Yes, it is rough and raw, and painful and cold, but it's also all so real. I have never felt more alive than I did during my few days spent in the earthly realm. Everything felt so *real*." She knew she was starting to repeat herself, but she couldn't think of a better way to convey her feelings. "The pain and the cold hurt, but it made warmth so much more welcomed. The hunger was bitter, but it made the food taste so much better. When my belly was finally full, it felt so much more satisfying. And the pleasure, oh, the pleasure was so much more . . . pleasurable. Especially the pleasure of making love; that was amazing."

Queen Danu smiled approvingly. "I'm sure it was. However, until this incident is forgotten, I would prefer if there were no more travels to the earthly realm. I'm asking you to remain in Avalee for the next ten or twenty years."

"Ten or twenty years!" By that time, Herrick would be an old man while she would hardly age. Would he even remember who she was, or would he cease to care? Surely by then he would have found someone else to love, someone else to make his wife and birth his children. It seemed so unfair, and yet she wouldn't deny him such a life; he was too good of a man. He deserved to be loved.

"If these humans are so loveable, as you seem to believe, surely you will find another to enjoy."

"I don't want another. I want this one," she wailed. "Why would it be all right for me to fall in love some other human twenty years from now and not this one?"

Danu's brows drew together sharply. "I did not say find another human to love, sister, I said find another human to enjoy."

"Danu . . . My queen, do you even hear yourself? Humans are people, each one is unique, like us."

When her sister's brows rose in disbelief, Sophie rushed on to say, "I didn't mean they're unique like us. I mean, like us, each is unique." She threw her hands up in frustration. "Oh, what's the use? I know I'm not making myself clear. And you've already made up your mind. This is all for nothing."

Her sister took a sweet, calm breath. "In that regard, you are correct. I am asking you to stay away from your Herrick and the earthly realm until you have learned your lesson. Perhaps, someday, if you still find the place so fascinating, you may return, for a visit."

Sophie felt defeated—worse than defeated, she felt unheard. Her sisters had not listened to anything she had said. They simply had refused to hear, because if they had, it was obvious they didn't understand.

Sophie stood and bowed to her sister. "May I have your permission to go now?"

"You have my permission to leave my presence," Danu smiled serenely. "You do not have my permission to leave Avalee."

Darn, the woman left no loopholes.

"Yes, my queen. I understand." Feeling frustrated and defeated, Sophie left the royal chambers to return to her own room where she would take a hot bath then crawl between the covers of her soft feather bed to wait out her time. Right now she didn't care if she ever attended another banquet, or ball, or party, or feast. Right now all she wanted to do was stay in her room and pout, and perhaps grieve a little over the loss of Herrick. She certainly didn't want to see any of her other sisters, not after the way they had conspired against her. If only one of her sisters had stood by her side, this might not feel so bad. But no, each had let her face the queen's wrath on her own. Not that Danu had seemed all that angry. Then again, Danu never appeared angry. As queen of the fae, anger was too far beneath her.

Out in the hallway she bumped into Adam, the queen's favorite, no doubt on his way to see her sister. Danu would surely tell him all about how Sophie had disappointed her and the punishment she'd had to impose on her youngest sister. The gossip would be halfway around Avalee by nightfall. It seemed very likely stories of her venture into the earthly realm would be told for the enjoyment of others after all, just not by her.

"Good day to you, Lady Sophie," Adam greeted her with a bow. "Did your visit with the queen go well?" he asked, smiling in that serenely smug way he had.

Sophie huffed. "You should count yourself lucky. She likes you. You get to do whatever you want."

Adam's smile faded. "Why the long face? What happened in there?"

"It doesn't matter. You wouldn't understand."

"Why don't you try me?"

Sophie shook her head. "Not now, Adam. You best hurry along. You don't want to keep my sister, *the queen*, waiting."

"We should talk later," he said with meaning.

"As you wish," Sophie shrugged, not caring if they did or not. If he were interested in hearing her side of the story, he could damn well come to her. She certainly wasn't going to go looking for him.

The only person she wanted to see was Herrick of the MacNicols, but she was no longer able to access his world, thanks to the mean-spirited efforts of her older sisters. She hated them for what they had done to her. It was wrong to feel such anger, but it could not be denied. Right now she hated her sisters and wanted nothing to do with them ever again, certainly not for the next ten or twenty years. High and mighty Queen Danu had requested she not leave Avalee, but she couldn't make her want to be here.

CHAPTER 8

Herrick awoke to find Sophie was gone. It was a bit of a shock after their magical night of lovemaking to have her wrenched from his side, but not all that unexpected. Though he had always known this was coming, it didn't make it any easier. More surprising was that she had stayed as long as she had. She was fae, not of his world. The idea they could have any future together was laughable, a fool's wish, and yet, his desire for her was painfully real.

It seemed as if only a moment ago he had felt her lying next to him in his arms, but now she was gone. Bleary-eyed, he looked around. She had left behind the large four-poster bed and thick wool-stuffed mattress. 'Twas still covered with the feather and down quilts and jewel colored silken sheets she had conjured, though now they were twisted and turned from the night of lovemaking they had endured.

Part of him wondered if it had all been some fanciful dream, wonderful and pleasurable, yet only a dream, but in his heart and soul, he knew it had been real. The bed and its covers were proof enough if nothing else. There was also the way she had healed his eyes, and then his body, and had taken root in his heart. The blessed little sprite had wormed her way into his soul, and he was forever changed. Afore, he had seen life as only drudgery and duty, whereas now he knew there was magick and beauty in the world if only he took the time to look.

Herrick pushed himself out of the big comfy bed and got ready to face the day. Sophie was gone, but life went on. The sun was rising, and there was no reason to lie about in bed while daylight burned. After he hurriedly washed and dressed, Herrick left his little cottage, closing the door firmly behind him. He stood for a moment, eyeing his mother's house. Maybe she would be up and available to prepare a meal for him. His time with Sophie had been grand. Better than grand, it had been heaven. But good times didn't last forever, and the better they were, it seemed, the quicker they were over.

As he approached his mother's cottage, the home he had grown up in, he could see her through the open window, bustling about in the kitchen. He opened the door without knocking then stepped inside. On the table, he noticed, were two mugs and a jug of mead.

"It looks as if ye are expecting me," Herrick said to his mother in greeting.

"Am I right? She's gone?" His mother had been bent over, stirring a pot of porridge. She paused from what she'd been doing, holding a large wooden spoon in her hand.

Herrick nodded. "Aye, she's gone."

His mother nodded. "'Tis as I expected. The fae are not known for staying long in this world. 'Tis not in their nature, and rare when it happens." She sighed and stared off into the distance for a moment afore she went back to stirring the pot simmering on the hearth. Focused on her task, she spoke to him over her shoulder. "From what little I ken of their world, I'm not surprised. Our world is harsh, and grim, and cold compared to theirs."

"Aye, Sophie said much the same," Herrick agreed. The few stories she had shared with him led him to believe her world was a place of beauty, and peace, and merry making—not at all like earth.

"I wouldna count on her coming back any time soon," his mother said as she gathered two wooden bowls from her cupboard. "Most likely she's had her fun, her time here is over."

Hard as it was to hear, Herrick didn't want to believe her. He wanted to believe his connection to Sophie went deeper than a mere dalliance. He also trusted his mother knew much more about these things than he ever would. She had the sight, all he had was a hurting heart and wishful thinking.

Though it didn't make the loss any easier, he understood Sophie's need to return to her own world. Taking a seat, he leaned forward and rested his elbows on the table with his chin cupped in his hands.

His mother stopped what she was doing to watch him with an inquisitive look in her eyes. "Are ye all right?"

"I'm fine. I knew this was coming." *I just hoped it wouldn't come so soon.* He tried to tell himself it didn't matter if she left today or a week from today, she would still be gone. She had warned him she would return to Avalee someday soon, and now the day had come. "She always told me she would leave, but I still hoped she would stay. Foolish of me, I suppose."

"'Tis never foolish to be hopeful," his mother said, her voice kind and soothing. She scooped up a bowl full of porridge and placed it before him, along with a loaf of bread. "Here, eat. This will make ye feel better."

Herrick poured them each a mug of mead to go with their simple meal.

"What will ye do now?" his mother asked as she joined him at the table.

Herrick sighed and gave it some thought. "Serve my clan, as always, I suppose."

"They need ye more than ever," she said, breaking off a hunk of bread. "We've lost our chieftain and need another to take his place."

Herrick took a long swallow of mead then wiped the back of his hand across his lips. "Why should it be me?"

"Because ye are Nicail's nephew. Ye are smart, and strong. But more important, ye are determined. Regardless what life sends yer way, ye deal with it and move on. Ye may not be loud or boisterous like yer uncle was, but ye are determined. I believe, in the long years ahead, that will serve ye better."

Herrick sat quietly for a while, eating and staring into his mug of mead. Her words were comforting, but was he strong-willed enough to get through this challenge?

His mother must have sensed his reluctance. "I understand ye doona feel that way right now. Ye have been through so much, what with the battle and the loss of Sophie. But give yerself time. Ye will soon be ready to take yer place as the leader of this clan."

When he still looked skeptical, she added, "They need ye, Herrick. And ye need them."

She was right. He couldn't turn his back on his clan. After he finished breaking his fast, he would go to the village and ask to meet with the men of his clan to hear what they had to say on the matter.

"The meeting will be this eve in the village square," his mother said as she began to clear away their empty bowls.

"Huh?" Herrick looked up from drinking his mead.

"The meeting of our clan, to declare a new chieftain, it will take place this eve in the village square." She washed out the wooden bowls and placed them back on the shelf. "I'll go with ye."

Herrick didn't need to ask how she knew about this meeting. He was sure she was right.

Though the task wouldn't be easy, someone needed to find a way to protect his clan from the unending harassment and threats of the MacDonalds, or any others who desired to abuse his clan. Herrick believed in working smarter, not harder. He also appreciated the benefits of a well-trained and honed body in fighting shape. And while he wouldn't back down from a fight, he wouldn't go looking for one to prove his worth either, much as his uncle had done.

When Uncle Nicail had agreed to lend his support to the MacDonalds in the raid against the Vikings, Herrick knew it was his duty to fight alongside his kinsmen. He also knew the loss of his uncle and two cousins was a terrible blow to his clan.

In Herrick's opinion, Nicail had been too eager to lend his support to Big Red. His uncle had hoped to show the other clans that the MacNicols could hold their own next to the larger, more aggressive MacDonalds, but he'd been wrong.

The MacNicol clan had lost three of their best men, warriors and leaders the clan sorely needed if they hoped to endure in these troubled times.

They were down in numbers, but they were not to be counted out. He would rot afore he would align his clan with the MacDonalds, and while he much preferred an affiliation with the MacLeods, he'd not go to them seeking protection, not if it could be avoided. If they had any hope for survival, the MacNicols needed to stand on their own together, or fall as one together.

His clan needed to finish building the keep his uncle had started, and they needed him as a leader, someone to take the place of the chief they had lost. 'Twas important for the MacNicols to stake their claim to their lands by building both a fortress and a keep at Scorrybreac that would serve them well. As a clan, he believed 'twas time they set down roots. They would always remember the struggles and hardships they had overcome, but now 'twas time for peace. *Generositate non Ferocitate.* Be generous, not ferocious. He would rebuild his clan, and would start with the building of a keep worth defending, where he would lead his clan towards a peaceful, prosperous future, and away from the fierce fighting of the past.

Skye was an isle of abundance, as Sophie had pointed out more than once. There was an abundance of fish, and his kinsmen were excellent fishermen. There was an abundance of fellowship and family ties to carry on the burden of building their keep. And most importantly, there was an abundance of rock with which to build. They need look no further than their own land to find everything needed to build a stone fortress and keep they would be proud to defend, and within which they could provide for themselves and raise their children.

It was time for the MacNicols to build their stronghold on the cliffs overlooking the sea, and time for Herrick to lead his clan.

CHAPTER 9

Sophie went to her private chambers and took a long soak in a scented bath. As she lounged in the steaming hot water, letting it sooth every blessed bone in her body, she felt no concern for the time ticking by. By their very nature, the fae had an abundance of time, and Sophie now had much more than she needed, too much. After turning herself into a sodden, wrinkled mess, she slipped between the silken sheets of her bed and closed her eyes to the world she called home, a home that no longer held the appeal it once had.

The Isle of Avalee, and the fae court in particular, was full of scandalous gossip, back stabbing insults, and deceitful intrigue. Humans were much more likely to use their swords or their fists to make their point, but at least one always knew where one stood with them. Here, her sisters smiled prettily then shot poisonous words at her the minute she turned her back. She felt betrayed. But even worse, she felt unloved and misunderstood.

It was a day or two later when she finally awoke, but still she did not leave her bed. Instead, she remained cocooned in down quilts and feather pillows as she stared out at the dazzling white sand beach and sparkling blue sky stretching far and wide beyond her windows. The scene was one she had always admired, but now it no longer held her interest; her thoughts were someplace else.

In her mind's eye, she recalled every detail of her time with Herrick of the MacNicol clan. A sad, bittersweet melancholy crept upon her as she thought about how lucky she was that Herrick had been the one she had found when she had chanced to look through the veil separating their two worlds. She recalled how he had asked for a boon and she had eagerly granted his wish to heal his eyes. That one simple act had enticed her to stay by his side, setting her on the path of her grand adventure. At Herrick's side, she had gone from being a naïve, judgmental, pampered faerie princess to a mature woman who had experienced the pleasure, as well as the pain, of loving another.

She'd had other fae lovers before she met Herrick, but not one of them had created the type of connection she felt with this one particular Scottish warrior. In ways she didn't fully understand, but totally appreciated, their auras had mixed and mingled and fused together to create a joyous bond, a joining she had not felt before.

Had Herrick felt it too? Had he been aware of their very special once-in-a-lifetime connection? She wondered if perhaps his mother carried a drop of the fae bloodline and had passed it on to her son; Mistress Mable did have the second sight. It was obvious he had enjoyed their love making, but she wondered how deeply she had touched his soul. Sophie had been too afraid to ask.

During her time in the earthly realm, she had also encountered the MacLeod brothers, two more examples of hulking human maleness, and yet she had experienced none of the feelings of desire she felt for Herrick. Her chance meeting with the MacLeod men had produced only feelings of disgust and repulsion, whereas Herrick was even more appealing to her when compared to those men.

She remembered the simple yet hardy meal they had shared at the Duffie home and the warm feelings of love she had felt expressed between Mary and her children. They were a family poor in material wealth but richly blessed in the love and comforts of home and family. She wondered if Herrick really would return to the Duffie cottage to collect the fabric being woven by Ellie. Perhaps he had already done so by now. Time between their two worlds did not always move in sync.

But best of all, she relished her memories of how Herrick had made love to her and together their souls had soared to new heights of blissful joining. Making love to Herrick, feeling his body and soul merge with hers, was the greatest experience of her adventure, perhaps the greatest of her life. It may have gotten her grounded for twenty years, but it was the thing she cherished most about her time in the earthly realm.

Why Herrick, she wondered. Why did this man, above all others, sing to her soul? Why was it when she looked into his eyes she saw the wonder of life and love stretched out before her? Why did the mere touch of his lips upon hers make her long for more, like a desert longing for rain, or an ocean seeking the shore?

A single, pure teardrop spilled from her eye and rolled down her cheek. She caught it on the tip of her finger and let it harden into an ice crystal. After picking a pretty glass vial from the collection on her shelf, she carefully placed the crystal teardrop inside and sealed its lid. Clasping the encased treasure to her chest, she began to scheme how she could possibly defy her sister's ruling that she not leave Avalee for the next twenty years.

Several days later, Sophie was roused from her bed, drawn by sounds coming from outside her window. Looking out, she realized the royal kingdom was preparing for Beltane, the celebration for the beginning of summer. There would be days of feasting and parties leading up to the final celebration of the bonfires at sunset, marking the passage of spring and the anticipation for a bright and joyful summer.

Perhaps it was time to shake off her melancholy and rejoin the land of the living. At least this way she could learn what her sisters had been saying about her. After slipping into a shimmery, ice blue gown that perfectly matched her eyes and made her pale skin and blond hair glow, she made her way down to the large banquet hall where nearly everyone in the kingdom had gathered.

As Sophie walked through the grand hall festooned with flowers, vines, and leaves, she looked over the fae gathered there, seeking out the smiling faces of her trusted friends. She spied several across the room and was on her way to join them when she felt the sting of angry eyes bearing down on her. Searching for the source of such hurtful energy, she met the sneering gaze of her elder sister Sindi sitting at a nearby table surrounded by her vulgar friends.

Sophie's whole body shivered in an effort to shake off the hateful glare. Sindi was known to be petty when she wanted attention but Sophie was in no mood for her sister's spite. Turning her back on her sister, Sophie started to walk away, determined to seek out her trusted circle of friends.

Above the din of the crowd, Sindi's jarring voice rang out. "My baby sister claims she fell in love with a human, if you can believe that. A stinking, smelly human. She actually spent several days with him and shared his bed. Now she thinks she can simply show up here at our most cherished celebration as if nothing has happened. The thought is too disgusting for words."

Sophie halted mid step and took a deep breath as she straightened her spine. She knew her elder sister could be cruel, but this was more than she had expected. What had she done to deserve such wrath, other than leave on her own to visit the humans? Was her elder sister really so offended by her actions, or was she simply jealous because Sophie had done something Sindi was obviously too afraid to try? Very likely, it was the latter.

As she turned to face her sister, Sophie considered what she should do. It was tempting to lash out at Sindi with both words and fists, but she knew it would do no good. She could never match her sister's ability to be nasty; to try would require her to lower herself to Sindi's level. That was a level of hell she had no desire to visit. As for the use of force, she was fairly certain she could best her sister in a fair fight, but it was forbidden for her to strike another member of the royal family. Still, forbidden or not, the thought held great appeal.

Refusing to lower herself to Sindi's level, Sophie believed her best course of action was to say nothing at all. She slowly shook her head in distain and breathed a heavy sigh. Her sister was throwing pebbles at a brick wall; she would not allow such hateful words invade her sense of inner peace. She turned and walked away to join her friends, hoping that would be the end of it. She was wrong.

"Is it true, Sophie?" someone in the crowd shouted. "Are Sindi's stories true?"

"Tell us what you did on earth, Sophie." another implored.

"Yes, tell us your story," said yet another.

She should have known attending the first social event since her return wasn't going to be easy. Waving her hand in disdainful dismissal, she said, "You should know better than to listen to gossip and secondhand stories, especially when they come from such an unreliable source. Sindi has never spent one day of her life outside the royal palace. She has no idea what she's talking about."

"I know better than to go and visit the humans," Sindi said loudly.

"You know nothing, and don't pretend you do. You only know what Adam tells you, and you believe every word. You're so gullible it's sad." Sophie made a huffing sound and continued on her way. She couldn't possibly hope to stop the rumors from spreading, the fae lived on rumors and gossip; she could only hope the people who truly cared for her wouldn't listen to such venomous words. And if they did, then they really weren't her friends.

Adam noticed the tiff taking place between Sophie and Sindi, and at first he paid it no mind. He was too busy, focused on pleasing his queen. A short time later, when Sophie got up and left the celebration alone, he began to wonder. It wasn't like the youngest of the royal sisters to leave a party before it was over, especially not alone. Much like him, Sophie had a natural talent for attracting a following and was usually seen with any number of her friends and fans trailing in her attendance. Based solely on his insightful powers of observation, it seemed her departure was not only hasty, but done in frustration. No doubt she had been stirred up by Sindi. Someday, that spiteful faerie would get the comeuppance she so justly deserved, he only hoped he would be there to see it. But for now, his thoughts were centered on Sophie.

He had been meaning to speak to her about her meeting with Danu, but the thought had slipped his mind and time had gotten away from him. It was understandable. During the Beltane festivities, he had felt it was important to stay near his queen lest some other fool fae take it upon himself to usurp Adam's rightful place of honor and prestige. He was not Danu's king, not yet, but that was all in the plan. It was a long, well-thought-out plan that required patience and finesse, and he had plenty of both.

As he thought about it, he realized he hadn't seen Sophie since their encounter outside the queen's chamber. He had seen Sindi, looking far too smug these past few days, as if she harbored some despicable secret about someone and was waiting to use it to garner attention for herself. He also recalled seeing Amora, looking giddy and goofy as always. The middle sisters Vanella, Quella, and Renalee were also in attendance at the celebration, bunched together as usual as if they were one. But until now, Adam was certain he had not seen Sophie.

It was highly unusual for the youngest of the royal sisters to miss a party such as this. Usually she was in the thick of it, listening to his stories and laughing along with the rest of his audience at his tales of human follies and foolishness, but not this time. It seemed Sophie had kept to herself since her return from her own little adventure. It made him wonder. What exactly she had encountered during her brief stay among the humans?

Adam languidly stroked Danu's long, slender body as they both reclined on lush silk covered cushions and whispered softly near her ear. "It appears as though your youngest sister has chosen to forgo the celebration of spring. I believe this may be a first for her. Have you also noticed her absence, or have I simply been too distracted by your beauty to take note of her presence?"

Danu affectionately acknowledged the attentions of her favorite paramour and shimmered from the sensation of his fingers dancing across her skin. It was a long moment before she answered. "I am pleased you should be distracted by my beauty, but you are correct, Sophie has not participated in our celebration."

"Are you not concerned?" Adam asked as he traced the sinuous curve of her hips.

Danu gave him a lustful glance. "Are you?"

He brought her hand to his mouth and suckled the tips of her fingers. "My only concern is for your pleasure."

She turned her head away, as if disinterested, but allowed him to continue his seduction as he placed kisses along the tender skin of her wrist.

"Do I sense unrest with my queen and her youngest sister? You've not yet told me what happened that day in your chambers when Sophie was there. It may have been the last time I saw her."

"Sophie is pouting, I'm sure. I've asked her not to leave Avalee for the next ten or twenty years."

"My stars, that is serious." If such a punishment were inflicted upon him, it would bother him greatly. He appreciated his freedom to come and go as he desired too much to let it go, although he mostly chose to stay close by his queen's side. Too many others would welcome the opportunity to take his place, and he needed to keep his queen happy. "What wrongdoing could she possibly have committed to deserve your wrath?" he wondered aloud.

Queen Danu slowly turned her head to meet Adam's inquisitive gaze. "She fell in love."

Adam flinched, unable to hide his surprise or his curiosity. Falling in love was never considered a crime in the world of the fae.

"With a human," Danu offered, her voice disturbingly neutral.

Adam nodded knowingly, understanding all too well the possible consequences of such actions. "Ah, that is serious. How did you find out?" he asked before moving his kisses up along her arm and to her bare shoulder. He had personally witnessed the damaging results when a fae fell in love with a human. If it were within his powers, he wished to spare Sophie such heartache.

"I felt the rise in her vibrational aura. It spiked so high it was easy to detect. Not that I cared, but Sindi came to me to report Sophie's indiscretion. She also felt the disturbance and alerted our other sisters, as if she had discovered something supremely important. Sindi insisted something had to be done. My youngest sister caused quite a commotion." Danu's secretive smile led Adam to believe she held a measure of affectionate approval for Sophie's actions. "Anyway, a simple request that Sophie not leave Avalee seemed the easiest way to settle the matter."

Adam wanted to know more, but it was important to ask the right questions without risking Danu's ire. "I can't help but wonder why you chose twenty years. Does it hold some significance?"

"Not really. It seemed long enough to satisfy Sindi's ire without causing any unnecessary disagreements. Of course, Sophie wasn't happy, but I suspect someday soon she will realize she doesn't need my permission to live her life. For now, her sisters still believe that to be true, and it's best to keep them happily misinformed."

"You are wise, my queen. Have you any idea how arousing that is?"

"Yes, my dear Adam, I believe I do." She cupped his face with her hands and brought his lips down to hers, effectively ending their conversation as they moved on to more important matters.

CHAPTER 10

Sophie sat on her balcony and drank the last of her wine. Her evening meal sat before her, nearly untouched. She simply wasn't hungry. The Beltane celebration was over, and she had missed most of it. She couldn't stand being in the same room as Sindi without wanting to pull out all of her sister's hair.

She had called for a servant to take away the dishes and bring her another bottle of wine, but when the door to her chamber opened, Adam was there, along with the servant, but Adam was the one holding the wine.

"Mind if I join you?" Without waiting for her reply, Adam made his way into her chambers. "I'd heard you were in need of an after dinner drink, although judging by what's left on your tray, it looks as though this is more about drinking and less about dinner."

"You weren't invited," Sophie said. She came in from the balcony as the servant began clearing away the dishes.

"Old friends don't wait for invitations." He uncorked the wine and filled her glass then produced another for himself. He swirled the wine in the glass and breathed in its fragrance before taking a sip. "Ah, sweet ambrosia, nectar of the gods."

"What do you want, Adam? Has my sister grown tired of your company?" She turned her back on him and took a seat on the sofa.

"Certainly not, but it's been much too long since I've had the pleasure of your company. You were absent for most of the Beltane celebration. I missed your charming presence."

Sophie rolled her eyes. She didn't believe him for a minute, and wasn't even sure if she trusted him. He was the favorite of her sister the queen and was probably here only to amuse himself at her expense. She took a sip of the wine and had to admit, if only privately, it was an excellent vintage, perhaps the best she had ever tasted.

"I'm sure by now, one or more of my sisters have told you all about my visit to earth, and my punishment. If you've come seeking details, I've nothing more to add. The wine can stay; you should go." Along with her servant, who was quietly slipping out the door.

"Tsk, tsk, tsk. Is that any way to treat a friend?" Adam asked, shaking his head. Uninvited, he sat on the sofa next to her. "I come bearing more than wine. I have information you may find interesting."

"Oh really? Have you made another trip to the earthly realm and need someone to tell your stories to? Don't tell me my sisters have grown tired of your tales."

"I heard about your visit to earth. The rumor is you fell in love. However, I don't believe in listening to third

145

party tales, especially from Sindi. I need to hear it from you." When she remained silent, he added, "I suspect it must be true. Why else would you shut yourself away like this? This isn't like you."

"How would you know? You're too busy being the favorite of Danu."

"I notice more than you may think. And I also care more than you may know."

This took her aback. "Why would you care about me?"

"Because other than Danu, you're the only interesting member of the royal family."

Sophie huffed out a breath. "That's not much of an honor considering my competition."

"See? Witty. I like that about you. Sindi claims you've fallen in love with a human. She's told everyone she was the one who detected your unusually high vibrational aura and reported you to the queen. Personally, I think she's more troll than faerie, but without you to tell your side, it's hard to dispute her."

"Sindi can go to Valhalla and tell her tale to Odin himself for all I care. I don't need to defend myself against her."

"Witty and defiant. Your charms never end." Adam paused and swirled the wine in his glass again before he took a drink. "You know, you *are* a faerie princess. You can do whatever you want. At least until you return to the human world. Then you must live by their laws of nature."

"Only if I don't upset the delicate sensibilities of my sisters," she huffed and took another drink of her wine. Suddenly she felt like talking. "You've gone to visit the human realm."

"Several times."

"Did you not find much to love, or at least appreciate?"

"It's different for men. I only go to seek adventure. For a fae male such as myself, earth women are easy prey for seduction. There's no sport in that. You, I believe, may have been looking for something else."

Appalled, Sophie shook her head. "Do you even love Danu?"

Adam placed a hand over his heart with a look of dismay. "Of course I do. She's my queen."

Sophie eyed him with skepticism.

"Perhaps not with a pure heart, but certainly with pure intent." He fluttered his lashes with mock innocence.

"To remain her favorite?"

"And to stay in her good graces. Quite a benefit to that," he said, smiling broadly.

He was honest; she would credit him with that—but such a cad. She looked down and noticed her glass was nearly empty but hesitated to ask for more wine. Around Adam, she wanted to keep a clear head, but that wasn't working.

"Twenty years, Adam—it's much too long. My sister is being cruel."

147

"Twenty years can be a blink of an eye or feel like eternity. How you spend it is up to you. If you stay hidden away here in your chambers, I'm sure it will feel like eternity."

"Are you suggesting I should go out and play nice with my sisters? I don't think so. While I wait out my punishment here on Avalee, Herrick grows older by the day."

Adam refilled her glass and asked, "Do you really believe you love this . . . this human?"

"His name is Herrick of the MacNicols, and yes, I love him."

His expression turned serious. "How can you be so sure?" he asked, sounding truly intrigued.

Sophie shrugged and took another drink of her wine. "I only know what I feel. Falling in love is a mysterious thing." She hadn't intended to say more, but leaning toward him on the sofa, she suddenly felt a need to explain what had happened. "It started with a look, a happenstance glance into the earthly realm. I took a chance because I wanted an adventure. Even when it became difficult, I was determined to see it through to the end. With each step I took, I knew I was walking deeper and deeper toward a point of no return, and yet I couldn't stop myself. There were times when I knew I should walk away, return to Avalee, and yet the next step forward was so much more appealing, so much sweeter. The greater risk would have been to walk away and lose the grand opportunity to see it through to the end. I was aware of the risk, and yet . . ." She paused, as if she had run out of energy.

"To not take it would have been the greatest risk of all." Adam supplied the words for her.

"Yes. Exactly." She marveled at how well he seemed to understand as she took another sip of his wine. *Blessings*, but it was good.

"Then you should return. You'll be miserable if you don't."

She looked up at him and blinked. "And risk disappointing my sisters?" Besides, Sophie thought, twenty years from now nothing would be the same back on earth. Herrick would age, becoming an old man while she remained young. It was very possible he would marry another and have a family, or maybe even die. She shuddered at such thoughts.

"Why do you care what your sisters think? Unless you plan to live your life trying to make them happy. And let me tell you, my little faerie princess," he said with a sad shake of his head, "that will never work. If you think you're here to please someone else, you can never win. But if you think you're here to please yourself, you can't lose."

It didn't surprise her he would say such a thing. As far as she knew, Adam thought only of himself.

She also didn't trust him. He had never been nice to her before; she could see no reason why she should trust him now. True, he did seem to like it when she showed an interest in his stories and asked him questions, but she always believed he would react as such to anyone in his audience who did the same. He belonged to her sister Danu, and that made him off limits to her. Just as she was off limits to him.

"Sophie, my dear little friend, don't you know? Can't you tell? Once you have loved someone, it changes everything. You can never pretend it didn't happen. Once you've plucked someone, human or fae, out of the billions of souls that surround you and made them special, they will always be special, at least to you. This man of yours, this Herrick of the MacNicol clan, can never again be of no importance to you."

Sophie's mouth dropped open, and she stared at him in speechless wonder. Where in the world of fae had *this* Adam come from? This was not the storytelling, self-aggrandizing, zealous lover of her sister who she had come to know and loath. This was a man of wisdom she might actually admire.

"But . . . but Danu has decreed I must wait twenty years before I can return. Who knows what might happen in twenty years."

"No, that was her request, not her demand," Adam said with a knowing smile before he took another sip of his wine.

"Excuse me! Did I miss something here?" It was obvious he knew something more.

"Danu told me. She *asked* for you to stay here on Avalee; she didn't demand it. It doesn't have to be that way, you know. Besides, twenty years is nothing to a fae. You can move freely through human time. If you want, you're able to return to any moment in their time that you choose. Although, I don't recommend showing up at the moment you left. It's best to allow some time to elapse; it will seem more real for them that way."

Sophie's eyes flashed open wide, and her heart began to beat wildly. "Why has no one else told me about this?"

"Because most of the fae care not one drop of sand more for one human over another. They rarely venture into the human realm, and when they do, they don't care when or where they go, only that the adventure is entertaining."

Suddenly, Sophie felt giddy. "I must be a hopeless romantic," she murmured into her wine glass, which was empty again.

"There's no such thing as a hopeless romantic."

That made her head bob up and Adam poured more wine in her glass.

"The very nature of a romantic is to believe in love. If not happily ever after, at least in long lasting love. And to believe in love is the most hopeful thing you can do, don't you agree?"

"I swear to the god Odin, you are an impostor. What have you done with Adam? The favorite of my sister has never spoken like this."

"Until you fell in love, my sweet Sophie, none of this needed to be said."

He had a good point.

"How should I proceed? What do you suggest I do?" Sophie asked, becoming excited. She could hardly believe she was asking Adam for advice, but in the last twenty minutes, he had suddenly, and rather unexpectedly, become someone she trusted, perhaps, even admired. It made her wonder why he was being so nice, but she stored that question in the back of her mind to deal with later. For now, she wanted to focus on how she could get back to Herrick with the greatest hope for a happy reunion. Adam had mentioned how advantageous it was to pick a proper place and time for her return to the earthly realm, and she wanted to know more.

"Where were you the last time you saw your Herrick?" Adam asked.

Sophie felt her stomach tighten. She wasn't very comfortable discussing such intimacies with her sister's lover. "I would rather not say," she replied hastily, vividly recalling her night of passion in Herrick's cottage. She was tempted to look away, out the window, at the floor, or even the ceiling, but she forced herself to hold his gaze.

Adam eyed her with a smirking grin. "Come, now, Sophie. You can tell me. I insist, if you want my help . . ."

She lifted her chin and narrowed her eyes. If she had to confide in him, she would do so with as few details as possible. "If you must know, we had just created the vibrational disturbance that alerted Sindi and Danu to my whereabouts."

"Ahh," Adam nodded knowingly. "You had just finished making mad, passionate love."

"That's correct," Sophie ground out. She was quickly becoming less enthusiastic about relying on Adam for his help.

"You needn't be embarrassed. We're both adults. But what I really wanted to know was, what was your man, Herrick, doing from the time you met him until you left?"

"You mean pulled back here by my sisters against my will?"

"Dramatics aside, yes."

"When I found him, he was lying face down on a beach on the verge of dying, and I healed his wounds. It started with his wish that I heal his eyes so he could see me better. I liked that about him right from the start."

Adam gave her a stern look. "You didn't change his timeline, did you?"

"Whatever do you mean by that?" Sophie leaned back into the sofa, away from Adam.

"Would he have died if you hadn't allowed him to live?"

Sophie relaxed a little, but she still held her distance. "Oh, no, I doubt that. He was badly beat up, but I believe he would have lived. It just sounded more dramatic."

Adam's stern look said he didn't approve.

"I mean more romantic, to say it that way."

His expression softened, and she saw a hint of a smile tug at his lips. "All right. Go on."

"I agreed to journey with him as he returned home. I even summoned us a horse. I thought it would be a grand gesture on my part to see him safely home."

"This is a grown man you're talking about?"

Sophie nodded.

"I would think he could make it home on his own."

"Well, yes, I'm sure he could. But he was still weak. You see, I didn't heal all of his wounds, not all the way. I rather liked having him dependent on me. I also noticed how much it drained me to use my healing power, so I wanted to be careful."

She had also liked thinking Herrick needed her. It would have made for a better story when she returned home, except now she had no desire to tell anyone of her earthly adventures. Except maybe Adam, and this was only because he was offering to help her return to Herrick.

"That sounds reasonable," Adam said. "You had never tried your powers on earth before. It was smart of you to be cautious."

Sophie liked the way that sounded, and grew a little bolder in her storytelling. "Thank you. I'm glad you agree. Anyway, we traveled together across the Isle of Skye to his home. It took a few days. We ran into a few problems." She didn't feel it was necessary to go into too many details of their time together. It wasn't as though she were trying to capture the attention of an audience at the fae court, although, there was one part of the story she was particularly fond of. "At one point, he saved me from nearly getting killed in a landslide."

"You were nearly killed?" Adam asked, sounding astonished. "That's rather rare for a faerie."

"Well, maybe not killed, but certainly bruised, and I'm sure I wouldn't have enjoyed that. But Herrick saved me from the falling boulders, and I was grateful." She gazed off into the distance and sighed, fondly remembering their time together at the hot springs, right after that chilling incident. When she realized Adam was sitting across from her, watching her momentary flight into dreamland, she brought her wandering mind back to the present. "Anyway, we continued our journey and eventually made it back to his cottage where I met his mother."

"Wait. You met his mother? Did she know you're fae?"

Based on his reaction, Sophie felt it was best she hadn't mentioned all the other humans they had encountered along their travels, although the McLeod brothers had never actually seen her. Now, she realized, it was probably for the best.

"Herrick's mother was expecting us. She has the second sight," Sophie explained. Seeing his look of concern, she added, "But I didn't tell her *who* I am."

Adam scowled. "If she has the second sight, you probably didn't need to. Who was this earth woman?"

"Mable of the MacNicol clan."

"Mable! You met Mable?"

Oh, pooh, this didn't sound good. "Yes. Why? Do you know her?"

Adam seemed hesitant to answer.

"Adam?"

"I've met her, briefly. But I didn't . . . don't know her well."

"What aren't you telling me?"

Adam shook his head and waived her question aside. "We all have our secrets. I'm sure there are things you're not telling me."

Sophie narrowed her eyes at him, but decided to let it go. "Fair enough." She took another sip of her wine; she had almost forgotten she was holding the glass and was disappointed to see it was empty again. "So anyway, now you know my story. When I was pulled back to Avalee, Herrick was at his mother's cottage and his uncle and cousins were dead."

"What? You never said anything about an uncle and cousins. When did this happen?"

"Oh, that was before I got there. They died in the battle that had nearly killed Herrick."

"Herrick's uncle, what was his name?"

Sophie thought for a moment and tried to recall. "Umm, Nicail, I think. He was their clan chieftain. I think he was Herrick's mother's brother, or something like that."

Adam scratched his chin. "Interesting. If I'm not mistaken, that would make Herrick the leader of their clan."

"How do you know that?" She looked around for the bottle of wine and noticed it was empty then wondered if Adam would summon some more.

"Just a likely guess. If his uncle and cousins all died in battle, that would leave only him to take his uncle's place.

Sophie shrugged. "I guess so." She didn't know much about how humans picked their leaders, nor did she care. "You don't happen to have any more of that wine available, do you?"

Adam rested his chin in his hands and looked deep in thought. He must not have heard her question.

"What's wrong?"

"I'm thinking Herrick might be busy for the next little while, adjusting to his new role as leader of his clan. I'm thinking it might be best to leave him be for a time."

That had Sophie worried. "But what if he . . ."

Adam's sly grin looked positively lascivious. "I don't think you need to worry that he's going to run off and find another woman to share his bed. He's been touched by a fae; it tends to leave its mark. It'll be a while before his body is ready to yearn for another, if ever."

"That's reassuring," she said with a sigh.

"Besides, you can afford a slight delay. It will allow your sisters to think you've accepted your punishment, at least for a while."

Sophie could tell from the look in his eyes, he was hatching a plan. She leaned in closer to Adam and asked, "So tell me . . . What should I do next?"

CHAPTER 11

Herrick took a moment to stand back and admire the work of his clan. It had taken several months of hard, back-breaking labor, but they finally had a fortress and keep they could be proud of. There was still more work to be done; there would always be more work, but at least the keep was to the point of being habitable without the constant disruption of workers marching through the bedchambers and construction interfering with the evening meal.

In the months it had taken to build the keep and fortress, Herrick had worked side by side with his fellow clansmen, and as a result, their confidence in him as a leader had grown to where he felt secure in his position as chief of his clan. He had gotten to know every one of the people he was destined to protect, even the young'uns, and felt as if each of them would lay down their life for the other. As a clan, they were truly united.

There was one exception. He had noticed one young lass watching him and his men from a distance, and yet every time he thought to make an introduction, she was suddenly nowhere to be found. He had once asked one of the older women about the elusive maid, but the laundress had little to offer, telling him the younger lasses had a tendency to move too quickly for her to keep track of them all, and nor did she feel it was her duty to do so.

After that disappointing encounter, he kept his curiosity to himself lest gossip begin to spread he was searching for a wife. Though she was no longer in his world, his heart still belonged to Sophie, and the last thing he needed was for some young lass to set her sights on him. Already, more than a few mothers with daughters coming of age had approached him to ask of his plans once the keep was completed. It had gotten to the point where he had almost welcomed the week-long storm that delayed construction and allowed him to hide out in his cottage on the hill. He claimed he needed to be near his mother to ensure her safety, but in truth, he had used the excuse of the storm to return to his cottage and the bed he had once shared with Sophie for one glorious night.

The bed and his cottage were much the same as when Sophie had left, with the exception of the bright and colorful blanket he had retrieved from Mary Duffie. Sophie had said she wanted this blanket for herself, and now it sat in wait for her, a strong reminder of her absence from his life. More than once he had been tempted to throw the darn thing away, but each time he had relented. He couldn't part with something Sophie had so highly valued.

On the morning when the rain and wind had finally passed, the sun shined bright in a clear blue sky. He was leaving his cottage to return to work at the fortress when he met his mother out in the yard between their homes, hanging out her wash. Leave it to his mother to be the first to take advantage of a sunny day. He was about to kiss her cheek and be on his way when he thought to ask about the mysterious lass he had seen down at the fortress.

"Ma, I wonder if ye might ken of a lass who I've seen watching my workers from a distance. I feel I ken everyone who lives in our village, and yet, I've not met this lass. I've wondered if she's an orphan or if she's been rejected from another clan and is seeking refuge. It might help if I kenned who she is. Can ye see her?" he asked, referring to his mother's second sight. He had also wondered briefly if she were a spy sent by the MacDonalds to report on their progress, but since his clan had nothing to hide in the building of their fortress and keep, he had quickly discarded that idea.

Mable laughed and shook her head as she draped a linen shirt over a rope stretched between two trees. "My sight doesn't work that way. It comes at will, without my bidding. It shows me only bits and pieces of what is, or what will be. I have no more control of the visions than I do a sneeze. I may ken when one is coming, but I canna control what it will be."

She finished hanging the shirt and stopped to look at him with her intense blue eyes. It felt to Herrick as if she could see right through him and into his future. A shiver ran through him, and he understood why some of the villagers felt discomfort in her presence. That was something he hoped to change. He was the clan leader. He wanted his mother honored and by his side.

"The keep is nearly finished. Can I not convince ye to come and live there once 'tis done?" he asked.

"What? And leave my home here on the hill? I think not," she said afore bending over to pick up another shirt to hang on the line. "I've been here too long to become one of the village folk. It may not sit well with them."

"I'm sure they'll accept ye, now that I'm their chief."

"I'm sure they'll be kind enough when ye are around. But even yer leadership will not stop folks from talking when the moment strikes."

She was right, people would talk amongst themselves whether he liked it or not. The only thing he could do was pay it no mind and not let it interfere with his ability to lead.

"What about when it turns cold? Can ye at least consider going to the keep for the winter months so I will not need to worry about ye?"

His mother took a moment to think afore she answered. "Aye, I may join ye for the cold, dark months of winter, but as soon as the heather begins to bloom on the hillside, I'll be back here to tend to my home."

Herrick let out a sigh and nodded. 'Twas a fair compromise. He was the chief of their clan now and was relieved to know his mother understood the need to respect his wishes.

"Besides," she added. "Ye will soon want to start a family of yer own. Mayhap with the mysterious lass who has caught yer eye." There was a laughing gleam in her eyes.

Herrick sadly shook his head. "It will be some time, if ever, afore the memory of Sophie fades so dim as to allow room for another to win my heart. I prefer to keep her in my thoughts a bit longer afore I let them slip away."

A bittersweet look shadowed his mother's eyes, and she nodded. "I understand. I still hold memories of yer father near and dear in my heart. I've no space for another."

"Not yet," Herrick said with a hopeful tone.

"Mayhap never. Now, get on with ye, lest yer clansmen think being a chief has made ye soft and lazy."

"Heaven forbid." He gave her a parting kiss upon her upturned cheek and turned to head down the path toward the village.

As he walked, he felt a pair of eyes watching him, but every time he looked, no one was there. He wondered anew if the MacDonalds or one of the other clans had sent spies to report on the progress of the MacNicol keep. So be it. Let them know the MacNicols were becoming strong and united.

When Herrick returned to the keep, he got right back to working beside his kinsmen to repair the damage brought by the storm. One of the walls of the stables had been weakened by the heavy winds and was leaning, about to fall down. He was working alongside Jonah, his newly appointed captain of the guard. They didn't have much of a militia to captain, but they had set aside a training ground next to the fortress and would soon begin drilling the men and younger lads of the clan. Today, however, they were shoring up the timbers supporting the roof of the stables.

"Have ye noticed a strange lass lurking about our fortress?" Herrick asked Jonah as the man steadied the beam Herrick was hammering into place.

"A strange lass, ye say? What does she look like?" Jonah asked.

"I really canna say. I've never gotten a good look at her, but I have the feeling we're being watched." Herrick swung his hammer high, hitting the top of the beam until it squared up under the rafters of the roof.

"Nay, canna say as I have," Jonah answered, heaving his shoulder against the beam as Herrick took another swing. "If a new lass was hanging around the village, I'm sure I would have noticed. Or one of the other men. A lone lass rarely goes unnoticed for long."

"Hmm, I'm sure ye are right," Herrick grunted, taking his final swing.

Both men backed off and eyed the beam they had just put into place. It looked straight and secure. Herrick gave the timber a shake and was pleased when it held firm. One more task completed, a dozen more to tend to.

"I'll tell ye if I hear anything, but I'll not be saving her for yer arse if I find her first," Jonah said with a wink and a grin.

"I'm sure I can count on ye." Herrick gave his captain of the guard a friendly slap on the back afore heading off to find his next chore.

The sun had burned through the clouds and was shining bright above. After hauling a cart full of hay into the stables to feed the few horses housed there, Herrick was hot and dusty and in need of a break. He strode over to the rain barrel at the edge of the keep and took a long, cool drink of the freshly gathered water. After stripping off his tunic, he took another cupful of water and splashed it over his face and chest, letting it run down his body.

From the corner of his eye, as he shook out his hair, he caught a glimpse of the maiden who had been dodging his attempts to meet her. He was tempted to turn and confront her, but past experiences told him it would do no good. She would flee faster than a sparrow could take to the wing. It occurred to him when hunting skittish prey, 'twas best to let them show themselves out in the open afore making a move. He needed to act as if he were unaware of her presence. Though he couldn't exactly try to hide himself away and hope she would reveal herself, he could disguise his intent.

Herrick continued to make a show of washing himself while trying to keep one eye peeled for the wary lass. He felt certain she was still there, but she was keeping to the shadows, just out of sight.

Afore he could decide on his next move, he was joined by Mary Catherine, one of the young laundry maids. She was carrying a basket of freshly washed clothes, and 'twas obvious she had come to flirt with him as she openly assessed his half-naked body. He, too, was momentarily distracted by the sight of Mary Catherine's wet bodice clinging seductively to her breasts. As he leaned sideways to get a better look, he noticed the concealed lass had actually taken a step out from her hiding place near the stables.

Ah, ha, he thought. 'Twas the attentions of the laundress that had sparked her interest. He wondered if she were envious, or merely curious. Either way, the ploy was working in his favor. Herrick leaned closer to Mary Catherine and asked, "How be ye faring on this bright sunny day?"

"'Tis a welcome relief after the storm. We've enough washing to last us all week." Eyeing the dirty shirt he held in his hands, she added, "If ye would like, I can take that and wash it meself."

Herrick gave her a half smile, as if taken in by her charms. "I'd not be wanting to put an extra burden on ye. Ye just told me how busy ye are."

"'Twould be no burden, Chief MacNicol," she said with a coy smile.

'Twas good to be chief, but he didn't want to improperly encourage the lass lest she think she had a chance of becoming the chieftain's wife and thus improve her position in the clan. "That's mighty kind of ye. I'll tell the head laundress of yer offer when I take her my dirty shirts."

Not surprisingly, her smile quickly faded into a pout. But he had other worries on his mind.

He had his back turned to the mysterious, hidden lass, but all of his senses were attuned to her presence. It felt as if the hairs on the back of his neck were actually rising up, trying to reach out to her. The muscles in his back tightened, and he rolled his shoulders, flexing his muscles to release the tension building there. Should the lass come within striking distance, he needed to react in a flash. Somehow, this game of cat and mouse had turned intensely serious, and he was more determined than ever to be the victor.

Glancing down at the puddles surrounding the rain barrel, Herrick got a glimpse of the lass in their reflection. It seemed her curiosity had gotten the better of her, and she had taken another step away from the shadows of the nearby wall. He turned slightly, as if to dunk his shirt into the rain barrel, but then leaped towards the lass, catching her around the waist just as she turned her back to him in an effort to flee. He held her tight, even as she struggled mightily in his arms. Though the effort to hold her threw him off balance, causing his feet to slip in the mud, he didn't let go of the maid. Rolling on his back to take the brunt of the fall, he held her backside to his chest, and together they dropped to the ground.

Mary Catherine scooted away, no doubt in an effort to protect the basket of clothes she had already worked hard to clean.

"Let go of me," the maid in his arms cried out.

"Not 'til I ken who ye be. Ye have dogged my steps for days. 'Tis time to tell me who ye are."

A group of villagers began to gather around to watch him struggle with the lass, but none offered to help either him or her. Jonah, he noticed, stood over him, looking perplexed.

"Have ye gone mad, Herrick, that ye must roll around in the mud by yerself?" his captain of the guard asked with a grin.

"It's the lass I told ye about. The one who's been stalking me. I've finally caught her," Herrick said as he dodged her kicking feet.

Jonah burst out laughing. "Have ye now? And would she be that muddy rag of a shirt ye'r clutching in yer hands?"

Herrick heard the tinkling of gleeful laughter and realized the lass he held in his arms was also laughing. "What's so funny?" he ground out.

Between giggles the lass managed to say, "They canna see me, Herrick. To these folks, it appears as if ye are fighting with yerself.

Though her speech seemed different, he recognized her voice immediately. "Sophie!"

She had stopped struggling, but now she shook with laughter.

He turned her over so she was beneath him and grasped her face between his hands, pushing back her wet and muddied hair. "Sophie, ye've come back to me."

Her expression turned serious. "For you, Herrick? I think not. Do you think you can flirt with any ole lass without me knowing?"

"I only flirted with her to draw ye out of the shadows, and it worked," he scoffed, defending himself.

"Aye, it worked. And now look at what you've done. You have us rolling in the mud like a couple of dogs."

From over his shoulder, Herrick heard the voice of Jonah speaking to the assembled crowd. "He doesn't look to be in need of our help. Maybe we should give him some privacy while he rolls around in the mud." Jonah's comments were accompanied by barks of laughter from the group of onlookers.

"Must be the heat of our sunny day that has muddied his thinking," someone else said, and laughter erupted again.

A devious grin spread across Sophie's mud streaked face.

"What's so funny?" he growled at her.

"I'm imagining how you must look to them." Sophie motioned with her chin as her hands were pinned beneath her. "From what they can see, you appear to be rutting about in this mud by yourself."

"Enough of this." Herrick scrambled to his feet, taking Sophie with him. In one swift move, he slung her over his shoulder like a sack of wool with one arm tightly clutching her legs and the other hand planted firmly on her rounded behind.

"What do you think you're doing?" she wailed as she beat her tiny fists against his back. "Put me down."

Ignoring her efforts, Herrick spun around to face his captain of the guard. "I'm going to get cleaned up. Have a tub of hot water set up in my chamber. Get one of the yard lads to help, if needed, but I want it there by the time I return." He then turned to walk away with Sophie's rump held firmly in place.

"Where are ye off to?" Jonah asked after him.

"To the bay to take a good dunking," Herrick called over his shoulder. Giving Sophie's rear a good squeeze, he spoke softer for her ears only, "And I'm taking ye with me."

"Oh no you're not," she said, squirming in his arms. "I'm not going to let you toss me in that icy water."

Herrick tightened his grip. "Unless ye are able to heat the whole of the bay, that's exactly what I plan to do, my faerie princess."

"But . . . but Herrick, aren't you glad to see me?"

"Thrilled. I'd be even happier if the others could see ye as I do," he said as he continued to stride towards the fortress gate. It galled him to think how foolish he must look to Jonah and the others, to be seen wrestling with empty air like a man gone crazy. There was no way of knowing how this would affect his standing with his clan. No one wanted a mad man for their leader.

If Sophie was unwilling to show herself to his people, what did that mean for him? Even though she was the one who had been spying on him for these past several weeks—of that, he was sure—her actions didn't indicate she planned to stay. She had already demonstrated her desire to return to Avalee once afore, and never once had she made any promises or indicated any desire to remain with him in the earthly realm.

He'd be damned if she thought he would leave his clan to follow her to the land of the fae. He could only imagine how poorly a human would be treated by her people. He would probably be viewed as nothing more than a plaything she had brought back to amuse herself until she grew tired of his presence.

With long, purposeful strides, Herrick marched out the fortress gate and down the narrow, winding path to the shoreline of the bay beneath the steep cliffs of Scorrybreac. Sophie had stopped her squirming, but Herrick had no illusions she would be willing to simply concede defeat and crumple to his command. More likely, he suspected, she was merely biding her time to make her move. Apparently, as long as he had a hold on her, she wasn't able to completely disappear, as she had that night in his cottage, but 'twas obvious from the curious looks he got from those he passed, he was the only one who could actually see her.

"Herrick, I understand you're upset with me," Sophie said as she hung over his back, "but Adam said it would be better this way."

"Adam! Who the hell is Adam? Nay, doona answer that. I really doona want to ken."

~~~

Sophie braced her hands on Herrick's broad back to keep from bobbing about as he made his way down the steep and rugged hillside dropping to the bay. "But Herrick, if you'll only let me explain," she began.

"Explain!" he roared. "After what you did."

"But you knew . . . I warned you I couldn't stay," she tried again before she was quickly interrupted.

"What kind of woman disappears without saying goodbye? Only the fae would pull such a thing, I am sure. We had just returned to my home; ye had just met my ma.

For Christ's sake, we had just made love, and poof, ye were gone. How can ye explain that?"

Sophie had to smile. Herrick was mad all right. He was nearly screaming with rage. What a powerful emotion. No one would rage this strongly if they didn't care so deeply. It was amazing to behold.

On Avalee, the fae experienced emotions, but never to this degree. On Avalee, everything felt more subdued, more contained, as if strong displays of emotions were distasteful. Sure, she might have pouted when she didn't get her way, but she had never stomped or shouted, not like this. This display of emotion from Herrick was raw and honest, and there was pure beauty in its intensity. She easily understood the appeal of this world to these souls who became human. Where else could they so deeply and wholly create such an experience?

They had reached the water's edge, and without breaking stride, Herrick waded into the gentle waves of the bay up to his waist and, quick as a wink, deposited Sophie into the frigid ocean before dunking himself to wash away the mud on his legs and torso.

Sophie came up sputtering. "How could you? You know how I hate the cold." She started to wade back toward the beach, but Herrick caught her arm.

"How could *ye*?" he shouted in return. "How could ye leave me like that? I know I'm human, and ye are fae, and never the two should meet. But believe it or not, I like being human. I'm chief of my clan and I have a duty to protect them as best I can. I may love ye and wish to spend the rest of my life with ye, but I have no desire to become fae. If that's what ye are looking for, I am sure there are plenty of other men who would welcome yer attentions."

"You love me?" she asked cautiously and felt a hint of a smile tugging at her lips.

Herrick stared at her in disbelief. "Of course, I love ye. I would have thought ye knew that by now."

Sophie felt a warm glow spreading through her body and was certain the smile spreading upon her face grew brighter. "And I love you. Why else would I have fought so hard to be here?"

"Ye fought for me?"

She nodded happily. "Yes, I fought for you. I disobeyed my sister to come here. My eldest sister, the queen of the fae. You're why I'm here."

Before she could say another word, he pulled her close and kissed her. It was fierce, and brutal, and oh so passionate. He held her clutched in his embrace, molded to his body. Heat rolled off him, warming her skin. She melted inside from the heat of his passion, dripping with lust, and love, and desire. Her heart sang, but her body shivered.

Sophie couldn't believe they were still standing in the cold waters of the bay. "Can we at least go back to the shore and dry off?" she asked when he ended the kiss. Thank the stars above it was a cloudless, sunny day and warmer than usual for Skye.

Herrick threw back his head and laughed. "Aye, my little Sophie. Always noticing the cold. It shall be the task of my life to keep ye warm. But as long as ye are here, I shall protect ye and care for ye and ensure no harm comes to ye, so help me God."

She had to catch her breath when he scooped her up in his arms then waded back toward the beach. "Can others see ye yet?" he questioned. "Or do I look to be carrying air?"

"Yes, they can see me. When it comes to magic, I can only do one thing at a time. I cannot remain unseen and summon those blankets to warm my body," she said with a nod of her head toward the shore.

Herrick didn't voice a word of disapproval as thick blankets appeared on the beach; he simply headed toward them, grabbed one, and then wrapped it around her.

With another wave of her hand, their clothes began to dry as she drew on the warmth of the sun. It was not something she could often do and believed it was his strength, or perhaps their deep, powerful connection that gave her such extraordinary magic.

"Come, let us sit and gaze at the bay, and I will tell you a story," Sophie said as she took a seat on one of boulders lining the pebbled beach. Herrick wrapped himself in a blanket and took a seat beside her, reaching out to enfold her in its warmth.

"I believe it is best if I start at the beginning." She went all the way back to that first day when she had been frustrated with Adam and had spied Herrick lying on the beach, battered and bruised. She recalled how she had healed him, as he had wished, and how she had decided to follow him home.

"It was your wish that started it all. I hadn't intended to fall in love with you," she confessed, "but I did."

"My dear Lady Sophie." Herrick squeezed her tighter and kissed the top of her head. "Ye are more than I could ever wish for."

"I only came here seeking a good story to tell my fellow fae on Avalee. But then I met you, and all that changed." She sighed, thinking how nothing had been as she had expected when she had made her first visit to the human realm. "You showed me what it really means to be human. You showed me how strongly you desire, how strongly you care for each other and those you love." She smiled as she recalled how kindly he had treated her, and Mary Duffie, and his mother. Each was an example of his kindness, consideration, and true nature.

"But when my sisters learned of my . . . well, of our . . ." Oh, this was silly, she just needed to say it. "When my sister Sindi realized I had made love with you, and that I liked it, I mean *really* liked it, she told our queen, and I was forced to return to Avalee. As a punishment, my eldest sister requested I not visit the realm of the humans for twenty years, and I thought my life with you was over. I had believed I was doomed to lose your love. I mean seriously, I thought it would be twenty years before I could come back, and we know you humans don't age all that well. But Adam, the queen's favorite, came to me and explained to me how I could plan my return. You see, Adam has been here many times before, and he knows how these things work. He was also the one who pointed out that my sister had *asked* me not to leave Avalee, but she didn't *command* me—a slight, but very significant, difference."

Sophie paused a moment, thinking of all she had been through, waiting until the time was right to return to earth, to return to Herrick.

"Since that day, coming back to you is all I've thought about. I knew it was important to plan well this time, and I saw how involved you were with building the fortress and keep for your clan. As Adam suggested, I spied on you from the shadows, watching for the right moment to make myself known. But before that could happen, you saw me, when no one else could. I think it means something."

"Aye," he laughed. "It means I missed ye and thought of ye every day."

Sophie's eyes grew wide, and her mouth formed a little O. "You did?"

"Never afore have I met another like ye. And never again could I hope to." He kissed her again, and she felt the familiar warmth she liked so much spread all through her body.

Her mind began to wander off to thoughts of their naked bodies entwined in the heat of passion, but the image didn't include this cold and rocky beach.

"Didn't I hear you order a tub of hot water for your chamber?" she asked, snuggling closer to the warmth of his body.

"Does that mean ye wish to return with me to the keep?" he asked.

"I don't think we should stay here. Not when your warm chamber and a hot tub of water awaits us."

"And when I bring ye back to my keep, for all my clansmen to see, what shall I tell them? That I found a faerie princess in need of a bath on the beach?"

Sophie gazed up at him with a sly gleam in her eye. "What would you like to tell them?"

He paused for a moment with a thoughtful expression. He appeared to be choosing his words well. "I should like to tell them I have found the woman who will be my wife, and she will live with me for all of my days. Can I tell them that, Sophie? Will it be true?"

"Are you asking me to marry you, Herrick, Chief of the MacNicols?"

"Aye, my love, I am. What say ye?"

"I could say I only came back for another grand adventure so I would have a good story to tell. But I can't think of a greater adventure or better story than one that begins with becoming your wife and ends with us living happily ever after."

"Does that mean ye accept?" Herrick asked, looking a wee bit confused.

"Yes, my love, my life, my Herrick. I accept," Sophie said. She was smiling, and laughing, and happier than she had ever been before.

Herrick stood and held her in his arms, twirling them around and around. "Ah, Sophie, I believe I shall be the happiest man alive, in this world or yers."

CHAPTER 12

Mable MacNicol hummed merrily as she sewed the tiny and even stitches on the gown she was making. 'Twas nearly finished, and a more beautiful gown she had never seen. 'Twas very likely the one for whom 'twas intended could summon something as beautiful or even better from thin air, but never could she match the love Mable put into every stitch. She paused suddenly with her needle in midair and looked up, cocking her head to listen. A visitor was coming who deserved her attention. She gently folded the gown and set it by her side.

A moment later, when she heard the knock upon her door, she bid him to enter. A man of pure beauty and grace stepped into her humble cottage. His hair was dark as midnight, his eyes crystal clear blue like the endless sky. With his long, tapered nose, high cheek bones and firm jaw, his face could have been sculpted by a master. He stood tall, easily over six feet, and his body was corded with powerful muscles.

"Welcome, Adam," she said.

"Hello, Mistress Mable." The fae prince greeted her with an unearthly smile. "I've come to share a drink of celebration with you."

She noticed the pack slung over his shoulder. "What have ye brought us this time?" Mable knew Adam rarely drank from the waters of the earth, preferring instead to bring his own liquid libations with him from Avalee.

"Something a little special, a bit of my favorite wine, to toast my nephew." He produced a bottle and two magnificently beautiful crystal wine glasses from his bag. Leave it to Adam to bring only the best. He set the glasses on the table, and after opening the wine, began to pour. "You're looking lovely, as always," he said with a flirtatious grin.

Heat crept up her chest, but Mable knew better than to be taken in by Adam's seduction. This was simply his way with all women of the earth.

"Off with thee, Adam. I'm an old lady, with the weight of flesh and the wrinkles of time to prove it true." She waived away Adam's compliment, though privately his kind words pleased her.

"Oh, but Mable, your light of love still shines bright. Therein lies your beauty. It's no wonder my brother took you for his mate."

Her eyes grew misty, and she blinked away the tears. "I still miss him, Adam. I shall always love him."

Adam nodded and reached out to cover her hand with his. "He made his choice; he knew the rules. Live as a human. Die as a human. Danu knows I tried to talk him out of it, but he wanted this life badly enough to accept all the limitations it offered, including a death that came too soon and robbed me of my brother. But he loved you, Mable. Of that, I have no doubt. And he loved his son."

"Have ye come to check on Herrick?" She drew back her hand to wipe the corner of her eyes.

"I've come to celebrate his upcoming wedding. Benedict would be proud."

"Aye, I believe he would," Mable agreed.

Adam gazed at her with a disconcerting eye. "You've never told him, have you? The *lad* doesn't know?"

Mable shook her head. "It was what Benedict wanted, for his son to live fully as a human." *To never know his connection to the fae.* But the blood of the fae ran deep in her son's veins, and she believed the faerie princess Sophie must have felt that connection. She paused a moment to smooth out the fabric of the nearly finished gown folded at her side. "He had nothing against ye or yer race," she said, referring to his brother.

Adam held up his hand to stop her. "I know, Mable. He simply loved you more."

"He loved being human," Mable countered. "I've not seen another with greater zest for life." Her eyes grew misty again, and this time she had to wipe away the tears. She thought she had cried enough for her deceased husband, but the tears, it seemed, had a will of their own, springing unbidden whenever her mind had a cause to think of her dear Benedict. But Adam had come to celebrate the joyous news of her son's upcoming wedding, and celebrate they would. "So tell me, what news do ye bring from the fae world? How is yer dear queen? Are ye still her favorite?"

"There can be no other," Adam confirmed with a sly grin. "She misses Sophie, but she wants her sister to be happy. Queen Danu is satisfied all is as it should be."

Mable's grin spread wide across her face."So I was right. Sophie is of royal blood."

"Didn't she tell you?"

Mable shook her head. "Not directly, but I could tell."

"Of course. Not much gets by you. You've been kissed by the fae."

"I had my sight long afore I met Benedict," she said, referring to her ability to see the unseen and know the unknown.

"You brought it with you from birth. I believe it's what brought Benedict to you. Much like Sophie was drawn to Herrick. But what about my nephew's wedding? Am I invited?"

"If ye promise to behave yerself, then yes. I would be honored to have Herrick's uncle at his wedding." And then, remembering who she was speaking to, she added, "But if ye breathe one word about yer brother to my son, I'll make sure Sophie reports back to her sister."

"*Doona fash yerself*, Mable. Like you, I gave my word. While there is much that can be said about me, and not all of it good, none can say I break my word."

Mable nodded in satisfaction. "Well, now, let me tell ye what we have planned."

~*~

One Year Later

Herrick held his wife in his arms as they gazed out through the cottage window to the heather on the hillside. They had come away from the burdens of the keep, back to his old cottage, to steal some time alone. They had spent the night making love, and sleeping wrapped in each other's arms.

"Are ye happy here?" he asked her. "I mean, I ken this life is not easy. Do ye ever yearn return to the warmth and sunny days of Avalee?"

Sophie shook her head and wrapped her arms tighter around him. "No, my husband. I do not. This is my home. My place is by your side. I have everything I could ever want or need right here. When it is cold, you build me a great fire to keep me warm. Thanks to Mary Duffie and her daughter Ellie, I have an endless supply of colorful blankets to cover our bed. And when I lie next to you, your body heats me in a way I have never known on the warmest day in Avalee. No, my love, there is no place else I would rather be. I feel like I am a member of your clan, and I have you, my love. At your side, your clansmen treat me like a queen, not with adoration, but with respect. Ours is a life of abundance. What could Avalee offer me but endless days of lazy boredom?"

Her words soothed his soul and made his heart glad. Maybe now was a good time to ask about her plans for their upcoming anniversary. "Do we really need such a grand celebration? It seems to me the wedding was grand enough to last a lifetime."

"Herrick, your clan is expecting this. A year of peace and prosperity has passed since that fine wedding of ours, and they want to celebrate."

"We could spend the geld on repairs for the keep. Or buy more tapestries for the walls to keep out the cold. Ye have said yerself, 'tis often cold and damp here."

"I've learned to adjust. And I have you to keep me warm when the nights grow cold. You aren't thinking of leaving my bed, now are you?"

"Never, Sophie. If I have my say, never in a million years would I leave yer bed."

She covered his hand with hers as it rested on her belly. "Even if I become heavy with child?"

Herrick stilled beside her. "Excuse me, wife . . . What say ye?"

Sophie turned and smiled up at him. "If I became heavy with your child, would you still warm my bed?"

"Ye wouldna jest? Say ye wouldna jest," Herrick demanded.

"I do not jest, my love. You are to be a father."

Herrick's arms clamped tightly around her until she let out a squeal. "Stop, you'll squeeze me in half."

He immediately loosened his grip. "My love, I'm so sorry. Did I hurt ye, or the babe?"

"No, Herrick, we're fine," she said, and he felt her relax against his chest. "But wouldn't you agree, we've cause enough to celebrate our first anniversary?"

"More than enough cause. We shall feast for days."

"And I can always summon more tapestries, if that's what you want." Sophie eyed him slyly.

"None of that, now. Ye agreed, no more magick. Ye live in my world now."

"Don't you mean our kingdom? Besides, I wouldn't break my word. I haven't used magic since the day we were married."

~~~

Sophie was fairly certain, other than her power to heal, she could no longer perform magic, but Herrick didn't need to know that. She had given up her life as a fae and now lived as a human, bound by the same laws of nature as her husband.

Herrick rubbed her belly, "If we have a son, as I believe we will, I would like to call him Benedict, after my father."

Sophie smiled in agreement. "And if we have a daughter, as I believe we will, I would like to call her Dianna. I believe Queen Danu would like that."

Herrick nibbled her ear, bringing goose flesh to her arms. "As ye wish, my darling. Anything ye want."

Sophie giggled. "You may recall, I was once the one granting you wishes."

"And thank God, ye did. 'Twas my wish that started this all."

It may have been Herrick's wish, but it had been Sophie's desire for a grand adventure that had made that wish possible. As she lay happily in his arms, she knew she couldn't have wished for a grander ending for her grandest adventure. She snuggled deeper into his embrace and said, "Enough of this talk. It's time for you to take me back to bed and let your body work its magic to warm my flesh."

She squealed as he picked her up in his brawny, strong arms and carried her back to bed. "Aye, my wife, as ye wish."

~*~

Nine Years Later

"Tell me again, Mummy. Tell me again," Dianna pleaded as she skipped merrily by her mother's side.

Sophie smiled lovingly down at her eldest daughter, knowing this was one story she would never grow tired of telling.

"It began on a beach, much like this one, where I met your father. He had been gravely wounded in battle with a fierce and nasty tribe of the Norse. Though he was on the brink of death, there was something about him that caught my eye and called for to me to come to his aid. So I left my beautiful home on Avalee and stepped through the veil of the unseen to come and use my magical powers to heal his wounds. He asked that I grant his wish to heal his eyes so he could better see my beauty, and I did, of course. How could I resist. Then I summoned a beautiful white horse to bring us back to his home in Scorrybreac."

"Raynor is grey," Dianna interrupted, referring to the horse they still kept in their stables.

"Perhaps he is more grey than white, but you will agree, he is still a beautiful horse," Sophie said, tweaking her daughter's nose.

Dianna laughed and pulled her nose free. "Aye, Mummy, go on."

"Well then, as we journeyed back to Scorrybreac, we fell in love, for as you know, your father is brawn and handsome. How could I resist?"

"Tell me again, the part about how you were once a faerie princess."

Sophie had told her daughter this story many times over and yet Dianna never seemed to grow tired of the tale. "As you well know, I was born on the beautiful Isle of Avalee and lived as a faerie princess. I still carry the bloodline of the fae, as do you. One day, you will feel it flowing through you and know you have the calling. All of my daughters, and your daughters too, will feel the magic of their heritage when the time is right."

Already restless to join her two younger brothers, Dianna left Sophie's side and ran down the beach singing out, "I'm a faerie princess. I'm a faerie princess."

Sophie smiled at her children as she watched them dance together along the gentle waves of the bay. Her gaze soon turned to her husband, as it often did, and he looked over to meet her eyes. He left the man he was speaking with and came to her.

"What was that all about," he asked, nodding at Dianna.

"She wanted to hear the story of how we first met."

"Again?"

"Yes, again. She particularly likes the part where I stepped through the veil of the unseen to heal your body."

Sophie looked her husband up and down. Such a fine body was certainly worth healing. "I often tell her how I found you on that Norse beach, far, far from home, on the brink of death, and saved your life to bring you safely back home to become the chief of your clan."

"I was on a beach on the far side of this island, and aye, ye healed my wounds, but as I recall, ye insisted on accompanying me home. Ye wanted a good story to tell yer sisters back on Avalee."

Sophie giggled. "I do love a good story. Especially ones with a happy ending."

"Do ye tell her the part where I had ye rolling in the mud because ye were spying on me?"

"Oh, *nay*, my love. I leave that part out. It's not very pleasant, wouldn't you agree?"

"I agree, we live a happy life."

Herrick gathered Sophie in his arms as they looked out to where their children were playing. Over his broad shoulder, she could see their fortress and keep standing strong, high on the cliffs above them. It pleased her deeply how, over the years, their desire for each other never seemed to fade. She knew she loved him even more today than when they first fell in love, if such a thing were possible.

Herrick cupped her chin with his hand and kissed her with passionate desire. "Maybe I should take ye in my arms and carry ye back to our keep where we can make mad, passionate love."

Looking up at him through lidded lashes, she teasingly asked, "Will you rip the very bodice from my bosom in your desire to make love to me?" Hidden from the view of their children, she reached up under his plaid and rubbed her hand up and down his powerful, muscular thigh, finishing with a firm caress to his bum.

"Keep that up, my lady, and I am sure I will," Herrick whispered huskily into her ear, his breath hot against her neck.

Sophie gave him a knowing smile then called out to the nurse maid who had accompanied them on their visit to the beach. "Jean Katherine, keep a close watch on the children. Herrick and I must return to the keep, but the children may stay and play a while longer."

"Aye, my Lady, as always," Jean Katherine replied.

"Jonah," Herrick called out to his captain of the guard. "Make sure they come to no harm, or it will be yer skin."

"Aye, my Lord," Jonah called back, bowing mockingly low to Herrick.

Herrick took Sophie's hand and led her back up the narrow, winding path to their home high on the cliffs overlooking the bay. It seemed the older she got, and the more children she bore, the steeper this path became. Luckily, she was still able to keep pace with her much stronger husband as he helped her along. Knowing that lying in bed with him would be her reward was motivation enough to keep her legs moving. Dreamily, she thought, as she followed her husband up the path, *'twas* another happy ending to another happy day in her truly happy life.

Laughing merrily to herself, she whispered under her breath, "And they lived happily ever after."

Keep reading for a preview of the next book in the
MacNicol Clan series.

A Time To Return

Book 2 – The MacNicol Clan Through Time series
A time-shifting romance from the MacNicol family
archives.

Tossed through time, a pragmatic Relationship Coach
learns she's not immune to conflicts of the heart.

What should be a relaxing vacation turns into a
working time-travel adventure when Teressa Ellers, a
pragmatic and gifted Relationship Coach, is swept back to
13th century Scotland by a powerful fairy. She's been
summoned to act as a matchmaker to secure an alliance
between two feuding clans. Taking the job and seeing it
through to a successful ending is the only way for Teressa to
return home – which shouldn't be a problem for the
relationship expert. However unexpected complications
develop when Rory, the chief's youngest brother, takes a
very personal interest in her and sets out to uncover if she's
a mystery to unravel or a woman to be loved.

Rory MacNicol is a handsome rogue warrior; unrelentingly charming, naturally old-fashion and completely unaware of her origins. She's an independent 21ˢᵗ century woman; witty, practical, thoroughly -modern and determined to return home. And she's about to learns that even a relationship coach is not immune to conflicts of the heart.

Magic took her back in time to unite a lord and his lady. Is magic strong enough to unite her with her own true love? A return in time may be the only answer.

"Love, 'tis the strongest magic of them all." - Rory MacNicol

A Time To Return

Chapter 1

Present Day

Teressa clung to the fleeting image of her sensual dream as it dissolved into the recesses of her awakening mind. Overlooking land and sea, she reached for the fierce Scottish warrior with broad shoulders, windswept hair, and smiling face, but he was fading away. *Wait, wait . . . don't go*, she called to the fleeting vision, but it was no use. He was gone.

Darn, she hated how her dreams always ended before she got to the good part. Unfortunately, her mounting arousal didn't fade nearly as fast as the dream, giving her a hefty dose of frustration. It was one of her typical flirting-with-a-hunky-man-and-just-about-to-score scenarios.

Lately, it seemed the unfulfilling endings were becoming all too common. She lingered a moment longer, trying to think up a happy ending to the fragmentary dream. Nothing came to mind, so she set aside the fantasy and decided to focus on the reality of her surroundings.

With great reluctance and a good amount of effort, she kicked back the covers and forced herself to shrug off the cozy comfort provided by the warm sheets. Stretching, she felt like a cat uncoiling from a long, lazy nap. And rightfully so, she figured, glancing at the digital clock sitting on the bedside table. Teressa had just spent nearly ten hours comatose to the world, recovering from a major case of travel overload. She was near the end of her vacation and had traveled a great distance to arrive at the Scorrybreac Village Inn in the small historic town of Portree on the Isle of Skye. After giving herself a few more minutes to contemplate her journey and savor the pleasure of having finally arrived, she rolled out of bed.

Still stretching as she walked, she went over to the window and drew back the heavy curtains to let the morning sun brighten the room. The Zen-like atmosphere of the sage-green room was perfect, even better than she had expected. Contemporary Scandinavian furnishings complemented the ancient inn, creating an interesting contrast between the old and the new. It appealed to her far more than the frilly or historical décors used by other village inns hoping to attract the tourist dollars. The Scorrybreac Village Inn was designed to be a relaxing, calming experience for the intrepid traveler who chose to go off the beaten path. It fit her perfectly.

Anxious to capture a few thoughts on paper, Teressa rummaged through her backpack and pulled out her travel journal. On the first page, she had written "Scotland, My Whimsical Summer Vacation." Several of the pages that followed were already filled with entries documenting her travels. She flipped to the next available blank page and began writing.

> *I arrived at the Scorrybreac Village Inn on Skye late last night. Lord knows the place isn't easy to get to, but it's worth the effort. I've traveled by planes, trains, and automobiles, not to mention the ferry that brought me to Portree, a picture-perfect seaside village on the Isle of Skye known for its magical legends. It's also a perfect setting for my get-away-from-it-all retreat. Now that I've arrived, I can get down to some serious rest and relaxation, and perhaps, if fate is so inclined, a bit of adventure. A handsome Scottish prince would do nicely, thank you very much. (Is this my dream talking or just wishful thinking?)*

As she clicked her pen against her chin, she thought of her mother and brother, Daniel, back home on the ranch. She turned the page and wrote a few more lines.

> *I hope I can entice Daniel to come here someday. It's too bad Mom couldn't come. I worry about her a lot more now, since Dad's passed away. I think Daniel would love this place. For some reason, it reminds me of him. Probably because it's kind of rough around the edges and rather old fashioned.*

She closed the journal and placed it in the top drawer of the bedside table where she could easily find it when she was ready to make her next installment.

Teressa undressed as she padded over to the small but functional bathroom to take her shower. While she shampooed her long blond hair, her wandering mind dredged up thoughts of Jeffery, her ex-boyfriend. He certainly wasn't the hunky man of her dreams. Too bad for Jeffery. If he hadn't behaved so badly at her father's funeral by abandoning her when she needed his support, he might have accompanied her on this vacation; but nope, that's not how it worked out. Grateful she had seen his true colors before she made a massive mistake, she let out a sigh. Love me, love my family was her motto. While the bracing spray of the shower rinsed all traces of suds from her hair, she reaffirmed dumping Jeffery had been the right thing to do. Resolute, she shut off the water with a decisive flick of her wrist then dressed quickly.

With a final look in the bathroom mirror, she took stock of her *au naturel* youthful appearance, which often had people believing her to be younger than her true age. She looked good to go, dressed in comfortable, well-fitting blue jeans and a light green T-shirt, and felt ready to take on whatever the Isle of Skye had to offer. After lacing up her hiking boots, she grabbed her full-length gray leather coat; she liked the way the long coat swung about her legs as she walked, giving her a feeling of rugged yet classic style. The twenty-first of June might be considered the first day of summer, but here in the Highlands of Scotland, there was a chill in the air. As the sun began its ascent across the sky, she saw the prospects for a bright day breaking through the early morning clouds.

In the lobby of the Village Inn, she stopped to grab some of the tourist maps and brochures of the local area. She was considering which sights she wanted to explore when she spied a purple-and-green plaid wool scarf hanging in the gift shop window.

She loved scarves and had a basketful of them back home. Besides being one of her favorite accessories, she figured a Scottish plaid scarf would make a great souvenir without taking up a lot of room in her suitcase. Giving in to her shopping impulse, she strolled into the gift shop and was even more delighted when she encountered a familiar face.

"Good morning, Lilly. It's so good to see you." She flashed a bright smile at the young salesclerk. Lilly had been one of her clients at San Francisco State University, where she worked as a relationship coach. She had helped the foreign exchange student maneuver her way through the world of San Francisco metro males. Lilly claimed they were quite different from the traditional men she had known on Skye, and she had needed help learning how to deal with the big city breed of men.

For Teressa, being only twenty-eight years old and the youngest member of the college counseling center was both a blessing and a burden. The way she saw it, she was close enough in age to her clients to relate to them at their level, while still being experienced enough to present viable solutions for the younger undergraduates maneuvering their way through what was often the emotional rollercoaster of college relationships. Her work brought her deep satisfaction; she was confident she had found her calling in life.

"Morning, Ms. Ellers. I'm glad to see you took me up on my offer," Lilly said.

"You know me. I couldn't pass on a friends-and-family discount." Teressa laughed lightly.

"Will you be staying with us for long?" Lilly asked.

"I'm near the end of my journey, but I'll be here for a couple of more days before I head back home. You know, Skye isn't easy to get to. I've traveled by planes, trains, and a ferry to get here," Teressa said, ticking off the various forms of transportation on her fingers.

Lilly followed Teressa through the small gift shop as she browsed through the collection of items for sale.

"It's too bad your time is so short. You'll be wanting to see the castle ruins before you go. I know everyone goes to Dunvegan," Lilly said, referring to a well-known castle on Skye, "but I've always felt the real magic is here at Scorrybreac."

"It's the first thing on my agenda. Right after I get a cup of coffee," Teressa said as she perused the display of postcards near the front counter. Again, she noticed the scarf in the front window display. "By the way, do you have any more scarves like the one hanging in the window?"

Lilly looked over at the window display and frowned. "No, not that I know of. It must have just come in."

She stepped over to the full-length shop window. "Must be one of a kind," Lilly said as she read the label. "Hand-made by Anne M. She's an artisan here on the island." She handed the scarf to Teressa.

Teressa ran her fingers along the soft-woven wool and then held it to her cheek. It felt so good, too good to pass up. "I'll take it," she said.

Lilly rang up the sale. "Do you need a bag?"

"No thanks, I'm going to wear it," Teressa informed her.

Lilly cut off the price tag for her then handed Teressa the scarf. "Zoey works in the coffee shop. Tell her I sent you, and she'll pour you a cup from a fresh pot."

"Sounds great. A fresh, hot cup of coffee. Yum." Teressa waved her farewell. "See ya later," she said, looping the scarf around her neck.

After introducing herself to Zoey, Teressa stood near the front of the coffee shop counter, admiring her new scarf while she waited for the waitress to brew a fresh pot of coffee. She was running her fingers through the colorful fringe when she heard a group of men enter the shop. From the looks of them in their rubberized boots and heavy all-weather work jackets, she guessed them to be local fishermen. When they got closer, their collective odor confirmed it. She waved her hand in front of her nose.

One of the fishermen, the tallest of the bunch, was busy trying to get the counter girl's attention, calling to her by name. "Hey, Zoey, make 'em hot and black, like always," he shouted.

Not wanting to lose her place at the front of the line, Teressa took a step toward the serving counter. Apparently, the fisherman wanted to defy the laws of physics and attempted to occupy the same space as her, causing them to collide as they each stepped forward.

Teressa stared up at the man, who was easily over six feet tall. "Excuse me!" she said.

The large brute stared back at her, as if she were an apparition.

"Excuse me, I was in line here," she tried again, moving to step around him. Unlike the others, he smelled of salt water and ocean breezes.

"What?" he asked, blinking.

"Where I come from, people are polite enough to say 'excuse me' when they're rude enough to cut in line." She stood her ground even though she had to tilt her head a bit to look him in the eye.

"Excuse me, miss. I didn't see you standing there." Spreading his arms wide, he bowed and stepped aside. He was still staring at her, but now he had a grin spreading from ear to ear.

"I'm glad you think this is funny." Teressa was trying not to crack a smile, but his grin was devilishly infectious. She dropped her arms to her side, relaxing her stance. He continued to hold her gaze with his dark green eyes. They were kind, and he had a ready smile. Maybe she had judged him too harshly.

"I see ye've picked up a wee bit of our local color," he said with a deep Scottish brogue.

It was her turn to stare blankly.

He reached out, touching the fringe of her newly purchased scarf. "A right fine choice."

"Here, Robert. Take your coffee and move out of the way." Zoey set a tall steaming cup of coffee on the counter.

"We've got a table over here," one of his buddies called out to him.

He picked up his coffee and raised the cup to her in a parting salute. "Have a nice day, lass." Still grinning, he turned away to join his friends.

"Sorry, miss, they think they own the place. Now, what can I get for you?" Zoey asked, drawing Teressa's attention.

"Large coffee with cream, no sugar," Teressa said, pulling her gaze away from the table of men. "Did I say make it a large?"

Zoey nodded, already busy pouring the coffee. "Would you like some breakfast to go with your coffee? Farm fresh eggs, and the cook makes a mean veggie scramble."

"You know, that sounds good. I think I will." Teressa took the last empty seat at the breakfast counter next to two young girls who looked to be sisters and an older woman she guessed to be their grandmother. She leaned over the counter and spoke to Zoey in a hushed tone.

"What's his story? How did he know about my scarf?"

"His aunt is the weaver. It's one of hers. Robert's the captain of our local fishing fleet. He usually brings his crew in here to warm up and get fresh coffee after a long night at sea. The younger one in the yellow jacket . . . he's my brother." Zoey set Teressa's coffee on the counter.

"Sounds like you know everyone," Teressa remarked, somewhat impressed.

"We're all family here in Scorrybreac," Zoey replied.

Teressa pulled out her brochure for Scorrybreac Castle and began to look it over. From the first moment she had heard about the castle, she had felt a strong desire to see it up close and personal; she was looking forward to her sightseeing adventure. While she was reading over the brief history of the castle, she became distracted by the little girl sitting next to her. The young girl, who looked to be no more than six or seven, went from tapping her spoon on her half-empty plate, to swiveling on her stool while trying to kick the legs of the older girl sitting next to her. Not surprisingly, the older girl was doing her best to ignore her younger sister, giving all of her attention to her grandmother. Teressa took one look at the little girl and immediately sensed her problem. Setting down her brochure, she turned to the younger girl, leaned down, and whispered, "It doesn't feel good to be ignored, does it?"

The girl's innocent blue eyes darted a shy look at Teressa. "No." She shook her head with pouty defiance and then looked down at the uneaten food on her plate. A glance over at her sister and grandmother told Teressa they had finished eating some time ago, and now the younger child was bored.

"Is that your sister?" Teressa asked, still speaking softly.

"Yeah, and Grandmamma. My name's Moe. We're going to visit the castle today," Moe said, also speaking softly.

Teressa gave Moe a friendly smile. "I'm going to the castle too. It should be fun."

Moe nodded but remained quiet, looking down at her hands. Her shyness was understandable; she had probably been told not to talk to strangers.

"You must be very special," Teressa remarked, trying to cheer her up. She took a sip of her coffee.

"Why do you say that?" Moe asked, still whispering.

"Because I see you're wearing purple. Purple boots, purple coat, even your bows are purple."

Moe reached up to touch the bows in her hair.

"Did you know that faeries and elves have a special fondness for the color purple?"

"They do?" Moe's eyes opened wide, and a merry twinkle accompanied her happy smile. "You mean, like the color of your scarf?"

Teressa glanced down at the purple-and-green plaid. "Yes, like the color of my scarf."

The grandmother and the older sister rose from their stools, preparing to leave. Abruptly, the elderly woman acknowledged Teressa's interaction with her granddaughter. "Moe, stop bothering the nice lady and come with me."

Teressa looked up as Moe hopped down from her stool. "She wasn't bothering me. Your granddaughter is delightfully charming."

"Delightfully charming?" Moe repeated in awe, all bright eyed and smiling.

Teressa nodded. "Delightfully charming," she reaffirmed.

Moe skipped merrily away, following her grandmother and her sister. When she reached the door, she turned to give Teressa a wave goodbye.

Teressa turned back to the counter just as Zoey was setting down her breakfast.

"That was nice of you . . . talking to the little girl, I mean. Here's your breakfast. Enjoy," Zoey said.

"Thanks. She looked like she could use a friend."

"I know the family. The grandmother can be a wee gruff, but Moe's a regular pixie. Can I get you anything else?"

"Nope, I'm fine. It all looks good," Teressa said, lifting her fork.

She was nearly through with her breakfast when Robert, the sea captain, sidled up to the empty stool beside her.

"Can I get a refill?" he asked across the counter to Zoey.

The waitress was ready on the spot and refilled his cup with the hot brew.

Robert turned to Teressa. "I hope I've been forgiven."

Teressa turned to give him a once over. He was easy on the eyes. "Yeah, you're forgiven."

He held out his hand. "I'm Robert."

She wiped her hand on her napkin before taking his. "Teressa."

"Lovely name. Have we met before?" He looked deep into her eyes.

"You mean like earlier when you almost ran over me?" Or had he already forgotten? She raised her eyebrows and smirked.

"No, I mean like *before*. I know I don't know you, and yet I feel as if I do. And yes, I know this isn't making any sense."

Teressa gave him a puzzled look. It was perhaps the strangest, if not the most blatant, pickup line she had ever heard, but she decided to let it ride. The poor man obviously had no finesse.

"I don't think so. I've never been to Skye before. Have you ever been to San Francisco?"

"I've never left Skye . . . grew up here." He picked up the brochure for Scorrybreac Castle. "I've been here dozens of times," he said, waving the brochure. "The first time, I think I was only seven years old, with my parents. It was strange, but it was like I could remember how the place looked before, years and years ago, when it was still new. I could picture the original castle, the training grounds, even the stables. It was like I remembered living there."

Her first reaction was he must have had a rather vivid imagination. Then she wondered if this were a case of bartender's syndrome, where a person would sit down and start telling a perfect stranger their life story. Being a relationship coach, she tried to listen without judgment. "Sounds interesting," she said.

"No, it sounds crazy, but what can I say. Every time I go up to the place, I have the same feeling. I've learned to ignore it, but it doesn't go away. Are you planning to go see it?" He was starting to look uncomfortable, as if he had painted himself into a corner and were looking for a way out.

"Yeah, as soon as I finish here." She took a final bite of toast before pushing the plate away.

He glanced down at his work clothes. "I'd offer to act as your tour guide, but I've got an oil leak that needs fixing. I own a fishing fleet, and I've got four boats I need to keep running."

Looking over her shoulder, she noticed his crewmen waiting at the corner table, watching them as Robert flirted with her. They were probably betting on whether he would score. She would bet against it.

"Tomorrow I'm giving myself the day off. What are you doing then?" he asked, looking hopeful.

Teressa sat back on her stool, considering his suggestion. "I don't know. I'm thinking maybe I'll check out Dunvegan Castle." She bit her lip, forcing back a grin as she silently recalled her dream of a Scottish prince.

"Okay," he nodded. "Then maybe I'll see you around." He took another drink of his coffee, draining the cup, and rose from the stool.

"Yeah, maybe." She shrugged then watched him walk away to rejoin his friends before her grin made its escape. He looked good from the backside too.

Teressa paid her bill and was preparing to leave when laughter from the corner table drew her attention. The one whose mirthful voice stood out was Robert, the sea captain. His robust laughter sailed across the room. It was the sound of unrestrained joy, one she didn't hear often enough. Though she had not intended to look his way, when she did, their eyes met, and she had a sudden unsettling feeling they *had* met before. She looked away, but as she headed for the door, she knew he was watching her.

Tricia Linden, author of timeless romance with a touch of magic.

In this lifetime, Tricia has lived in five states, on two islands, and on a farm, and is now living with her soulmate in Northern California. Her travels have taken her to Canada, Mexico, Australia, Hong Kong, Guam, England, Scotland, several countries in Europe, and several states in the US. Besides her love of reading and writing romance, she has a great fondness for Pink Flamingos. Over the years, she's gathered a rather large collection of the fun pink birds.

Website: https://tricia-linden.com/

Facebook: https://www.facebook.com/TriciaLindenAuthor/

Tweeter: @TriciaLinden69

Email: Tricia.Linden@ymail.com

www.ingramcontent.com/pod-product-compliance
Lightning Source LLC
Chambersburg PA
CBHW020822150626

46554CB00016B/382